Lloyd Z. Remick, Esquire concentrates his practice in the areas of entertainment, sports, hospitality and communications law. He is also President of Zane Management, Inc., a Philadelphia based sports, entertainment and communications consulting and management firm. Mr. Remick received his B.S. from Wharton School in 1959, his J.D. from Temple University School of Law in 1962, and a L.L.M. in tax law from Villanova School of Law in 1984.

Mr. Remick represents several award winning recording artists, writers, and producers, as well as a number of television, radio, and entertainment personalities. In addition, he represented and managed the late Grammy Award winning Grover Washington, Jr. for over 20 years and 4-time Grammy singer, producer and recording artist Bunny Sigler for over 40 years. Mr. Remick has been a registered contract adviser with the National Football League Players' Association and the NCAA. He has also represented athletes in variety of other sports, including basketball, baseball, ice-skating, crew, boxing, soccer, and track and field. He has been elected by his peers to include "Super Lawyers"; "Best Lawyers in America" and Internationl Entertainment Lawyer of the Year.

Dedication

To my lovely wife Cynthia and children John, Brad, Pam, Lauren, Jennifer and Jack for sharing the highs, lows and sometime sideways adventures of my law career. Sorry for the missed games and recitals while I was away with clients.

To my close and dear client and friend four-time Grammy recording artist, writer and producer Walter "Bunny" Sigler who on October 6th, 2017 took his music and singing to a higher level. Rest in peace.

To the many men and women, creative-types, God given talents who wish to be a "superstar". It takes three things to be a "star": talent, luck, and contacts, so never stop striving and reaching for your goals.

Lloyd Zane Remick

TWO TIMES PLATINUM

AUSTIN MACAULEY PUBLISHERS™

London • Cambridge • New York • Sharjah

Copyright © Lloyd Zane Remick (2017)

Ordering Information:
Quantity sales: special discounts are available on quantity purchases by corporations, associations, and others. For details, contact the publisher at the address below.

ISBN 9781947353893 (Paperback)
ISBN 9781947353886 (Hardback)
ISBN 9781947353879 (E-Book)

1. The main category of the book — Crime & Mystery

www.austinmacauley.com/us

First Published (2017)
Austin Macauley Publishers™ LLC
40 Wall Street, 28th Floor
New York, NY 10005
USA

mail-usa@austinmacauley.com
+1 (646) 5125767

Acknowledgments

Life is a continual learning curve of experiences, so I thank all of the many professors, mentors, interns, associates and partners who have aided in my learning curve and enabled me to write this novel.

A thank you to Brent Vasher, Esquire and Alissa Kontanis for their assistance in computer and technology help for someone who did not grow up using these devices.

Much appreciation to Chris J. Cabott, Esquire and Kaitlyn M. O'Neill, Esquire for assisting and helping me with much of the legal work in our office when I needed time to finish Two Times Platinum.

To long time friend Kevin Roth, singer, songwriter and recording artist who penned the wonderful lyrics to the song "Come In Out of the Rain."

A general thank you to all my clients and associates who have been so loyal and have helped me learn from their experiences.

A special thanks to the personnel at Austin Macauley Publishers and to the wonderful patience and help from Ashley Pascual, Editorial Assistant, Jade Robertson, International Publishing Director, and especially Mark Grants, with whom I have had the pleasure of working with closely.

Chapter One

"So you want to be a star?" Dex Randle laughed as he shifted in his old but comfortable chair. A relic from the past, the chair was oversized and outdated; however, Dex couldn't break a tradition he learned long ago. He remembered receiving advice some 25 years prior from his crafty old mentor, "Always sit in an imposing large chair, look down upon your client, and you can charge more. If your client is taller than you, sit on the edge of the desk."

Yeah, Dex thought, *can't even charge my normal rate of $400 per hour on this deal. Gotta go contingent, but what the hell? Been doing that most of my life. Maybe this client will be the one, a monster act.*

All managers and entertainment lawyers go searching the world over for that one great act, and that brisk autumn day sitting across the desk, maybe three feet away, was the best voice combined with great looks Dex had seen or heard in a very long time.

"Can you help me with this management contract, and should I sign?" Val Clifton's raspy voice seemed to float through the air and have a body of its own.

Dex studied the beautiful recording artist wannabe, peering into her violet and piercing eyes, which seemed to look into his very soul.

If she could read his mind at that very moment, he would be embarrassed.

Entertainment lawyers by their very nature can ask enough questions to confuse a saint. Dex bombarded her with questions.

"How did you meet this guy?"

"Has he ever seen you perform live?"

"Does he have industry contacts, and can he get you a record deal?"

"Will he put his money where his mouth is?"

"What about getting you an agent so you can have gigs?"

"Can he get you a top producer who can make magic with your voice and the right song?"

Val put up her hand indicating he should slow down, then sat ready for his advice and lecture. Dex was almost on autopilot for lecture 101—how the industry was tough on newcomers, how everyone in it was glib, fast-talking and always ready to pounce on the innocent and take advantage. This was one innocent lady who would be grabbed up by the parasites without some guiding hand.

"Let me review the contract, suggest some changes, do some due diligence on this guy and you can call my office on Monday after eleven."

She stood, stretched and watched Dex follow her movement, smiled with those piercing violet eyes, extended her hand for him to shake, and then nodded good-bye.

This lady was trouble, and Dex scratched the scribbled word *innocent* off his yellow tablet and smiled back.

Dex was in his forties, young looking for his age, and had years of martial arts training, both physical and mental, that conditioned him to appear relaxed. Comfortable with his own being, he was outwardly friendly and easy to be with, but it hid a keen awareness of his surroundings. Hidden was a deep wariness of people and what they said, more important was what they did.

He really understood the heart of the warrior and spent much of his time conditioning his mind and body to remain under control.

"Never let the other side know all of what you are thinking, appear to help them to achieve their purpose just so long as you achieve what you want. Never think one move at a time, rather plan several moves ahead of your opponent," Dex quietly said beneath his breath.

Be like water. How many times had he heard his sensei say that? Flow and be adaptable.

"Water conforms to what contains it. It knows no size nor limitation, other than where you put it. You change shape and direction in a negotiation as water changes shape," he said. "You confront your enemy smiling but at a second you can change to be deadly serious."

The ring of the intercom startled Dex. This was going to be a heck of a good day.

"Prof," Sara, his third-year law student who had a slight British accent, intoned into the intercom.

"I've got a Sammy, sounds like lethal or something like that, on the phone asking for you."

"Don't know him. What's he want?"

"Wouldn't say."

"Okay, put him through."

11

"Mr. Randle, they call me Sammy—Sammy the Lethal. Mr. Carpozzi says I'm to pick up the papers now. Like right now, pronto."

"Excuse me? Do I know you?"

"Not important. What is important is if Mr. Carpozzi says now, he means now, and I'm on my way over to your office," he said, then the phone went dead.

"Hey, what's going on? Who is this Caroza or Carpoiti or whatever his name is? What papers? Sara, come in here, now please." Dex looked up and towards the door.

"Yes, Prof, what do you need?"

"Do we know this guy on the phone or a Mr. Caroza?"

"It's Carpozzi." She smiled and handed Dex Thursday's Philadelphia *Daily News,* the city newspaper with the headline CARPOZZI PURCHASES CTIWY RECORD CO.

A long article followed detailing Carpozzi and his alleged ties to some criminal enterprises and certain organized crime figures. The article detailed Carpozzi's takeover of Can't Take It with You Records as president and CEO.

Sara looked at her boss as he read the article and shifted slightly in her chair, letting out her breath. Her blouse tightened as Dex looked up and his eyes moved involuntarily to her chest.

They both laughed and Dex told her to pack up her bag so he could give her a lift to class and on the way they would discuss the call.

Chapter Two

Dex eased his two-seater Lexus out of his reserved spot and turned north toward the law school, where he was an adjunct professor teaching entertainment law to second- and third-year students.

Sara chattered on about something or other, but Dex was already lost in his own thoughts. It was a bunch of bull about those who can do and the others teach. Two of his close friends had given up the fast-paced world of private practice, feeling burned out and unfulfilled. They were now the happiest of his friends. He often wondered why he taught. It definitely wasn't for the money. Maybe it was the give and take of trading with young minds or the control factor. Control? He laughed at the thought. A year before, a young associate in a moment of anger or perhaps honesty told Dex guys like him teach as part ego and a part control.

Was it control? It did make him feel good to lecture, almost like being an actor on stage or opening in front of a jury and gaining the jurors' attention, each person hanging on every word. Power did feel good, he thought as a pair of violet eyes entered his mind. He thought about how just a few hours before he'd had his meeting with Ms. Violet Eyes, then his thoughts quickly shifted to the menacing phone call that followed. He wondered if and how they were connected.

"I wonder if that guy Sammy ever showed at my office. Oh well, tomorrow is another day," Dex mumbled to himself.

"What did you say, Prof?" Sara chirped.

"Nothing important. Let's go." They pulled into the reserved space for faculty, parked and proceeded up the path to the law school and into classroom 305. The eager students were already in their seats as Dex walked to the lectern.

"So, Professor Randle, what about T.O. And McNabb? Will they ever get it together?" piped a voice from the third row, referring to the unsettled status of two football players.

"Not in this lifetime. Football teams like armies or law firms must learn to subvert the individual ID to the team effort or it all doesn't mesh. We've all heard there is no letter 'I' in the word *team,* and life is like an assembly line. When everyone is moving in sync, it's like being in a zone. When a part goes awry, it all breaks down."

"What about his salary? Can they cut it for failure for conduct unbecoming?"

"Well, Jon, what do you think?"

Dex loved to take questions directed at him and turn them back on the students. The very essence of law school training was to question everything and learn from self-doubt and then learn to reason and hopefully search and find the truth. Socrates had it right in raising questions in his eternal search for the truth. Good professors didn't spoon-feed every answer but tried to instill a hunger for searching and desire for learning.

The class went well and after answering a few after-class questions, Dex heard his cell phone ring with one of his client's ring tones blaring away.

"Hello?"

"Don't ever do that again. Where's the contract?"

The voice needed no introduction. "Been teaching." *Why am I explaining anything to this jerk?* Dex thought but knew better than to say it out loud.

"Meet you at your office in 15 minutes, and don't be late."

"Hey, how did you get this private number?"

The only answer was the dead sound of the phone. Dex unhappily made a U-turn and headed back towards the office.

As he stepped off the elevator, Nora, his receptionist said, "Mr. Randle, some guys are in your office. Should I call security? They said you were expecting them, and I couldn't stop them and didn't know what to do."

"It's okay, Nora. Thanks," Dex said as he walked down the hall. He felt an uneasiness in his solar plexus, like someone planting a shot in a ball game or an unexpected punch in the stomach.

In his office, on his back couch, sat a character that looked like he was out of a gangster movie, complete with sunglasses, chains and a body that could play defensive tackle on any team in the NFL.

On a chair in front of his desk sat a slightly heavy well-dressed man with a perfectly starched white shirt, dark tie and very expensive gold-and-diamond cufflinks shaped like dice.

"Good evening, Mr. Randle. I trust your class went well."

There was no mistaking the voice—thick accent, cold and emotionless. Dex had heard it many times on TV, always on the news segment.

"Mr. Carpozzi, how are you, and what brings you to my office?"

15

"Val Clifton. You are going to represent her," came the reply. "I was told you're the best, and I only deal with the best."

"Thanks...but I haven't made up my mind as to whether I am representing her yet. Carpozzi raised his hand to cut Dex off mid-sentence.

"Sammy here will be her manager. She's going to sign a management contract, then she'll soon be signing a record contract. You'll be involved in that also."

Carpozzi reached into his jacket pocket and pulled out a thick envelope and gently pushed it to the top of a pile of papers on Dex's desk, never taking his eyes from him.

"Take care of this first thing in the morning. Sammy will call you."

He rose, straightened his jacket as the mountain jumped to get the door without another word. Dex sat in his big chair, stared at the envelope and recalled his earlier thoughts on being in control.

"Wow, first meeting and I lose control. Chalk one up for the other side," he said to no one in particular.

Chapter Three

Dinner at the Randle home was a fun event. The two kids Bret, 11, and 15 year-old James were all boys, having lean-in build like their father and chiseled features like their mother, Donna. Bret was tough and questioned everything; Jamie was more easygoing, smart but casual in his approach to life.

Dex spent whatever time he could with his sons, believing quality time was even more important than quantity. The family interacted with activities like ball games, target shooting with air guns, and dinner, especially dinner. After the encounter with Carpozzi, Dex looked forward to a relaxing and informal dinner with Donna and the kids.

"So how was school?" Dex, asked no one in particular.

"Okay," they both answered in unison.

Dex turned to his wife, smiled, and sipped at his nightly glass of red wine, usually merlot. Donna swiftly and deftly portioned the take-out dinner of spare ribs and mashed potatoes. Donna was a good cook but cooking for her family wasn't much appreciated. She had vainly tried to instill an appreciation for fine food but found greater success with casual menus. The boys took turns doing the dishes while their parents enjoyed a few minutes alone at the table drinking coffee and speaking about the day's events.

Then Dex would usually go into his study, a retreat with a large-screen HDTV, surround sound, books everywhere and a shelf full of trophies. Among his numerous tennis and football trophies, the one Dex was most proud of was a four foot silver martial arts figure from his triumph in a tri-state black belt tournament. Dex believed every man needed his own cave or retreat, a place where he could unwind and think through his day and contemplate that which was to come. Amongst these outward trappings representing just an instance of personal achievements, he could discard them and focus on what was really important to him—family, friends and clients.

The books on his table next to his desk were a composite of his being. *The Art of War* by Sun Tzu, the Chinese general who wrote of war, and how to plan and plot overcoming an adversary, which Dex often read and reread, three books on philosophy, and law books on movie law, record contracts and sports law.

The study had an elaborate sound system that was used to listen to music client demos and, of course, the large HDTV.

"Better think about that management contract and what I want it to convey," he muttered. "Fifteen percent commission is plenty for that Sammy mountain man, and who would want to be tied to him anyway? Perhaps a one-year term and if he gets Val a good record deal with cash advances and a good royalty rate and nationwide distribution of her records, then he can have a two-year option to extend the contract. While I'm at it, I'll exclude production costs while making the record from management commissions." He jotted notes for later inclusion. "Oh yes, don't give him any ownership of any writers or publishing shares in case she wrote songs." Many managers want to share in a percentage of songs written by their client but Dex tried to avoid doing so. He thought, *If I gotta get involved then damn. I'm gonna do a good job for her, she's my client, and the heck with Carpozzi.*

He tried not to think about the thick, white envelope that had been placed on his desk and contained 50 hundred-dollar bills and where it came from.

Upstairs, he heard his wife walking toward the bedroom, and his thoughts turned to his beautiful Donna, then back to the notes for the management contract. Time enough for that later.

Jamie came in and slid next to his dad and asked, "Whatcha doing?" Without waiting for an answer, he showed Dex a picture of him with his teammates dressed in their hockey uniforms. Dex hugged Jamie and told him how proud he was of him making varsity in his freshman year of high school, and promised he would be at all the home games.

"Study hard, 'cause college is important. A scholarship for hockey would be great, but there's more to life than sports. You want to be a good person. Don't forget, being respected by your buddies is also part of a man's character. The test of a man is his character and keeping his word."

"I got it, Dad. Love ya. Later," Jamie said as he bounced up the study steps. Dex noted a few more points on his yellow pad and his thoughts again turned to Donna as he turned off the lights and bounded upstairs.

The morning sun lit the bedroom and Dex stumbled to the bathroom for his daily stretching and balancing exercises. He challenged himself to see how long he could stand on one foot with his eyes closed. Twenty, thirty, yes thirty-five seconds.

19

He was going to beat old man time. One of the health books he's read said if a man could balance on one foot for 30 seconds with his eyes closed, he had the balance of a thirty-year-old in good health. Dex practiced every morning.

Donna and the kids were already eating breakfast and in conversation as Dex got his juice and black coffee, drank them and blew a kiss to the kids, hugged Donna and was out the door.

"Morning, Mr. R. Here are your messages, and that man Sammy has called at least three times already. He sure isn't polite on the phone." Nora, his office receptionist made a face as she handed him the last message.

Dex opened the door to his office, tossed his stuff on his desk then leaned back in his chair as the phone rang. Dex didn't have to guess who it was.

"Got your client Val in the car, and we'll be at your office in 15 minutes."

"Take her to breakfast and make it an hour and the contracts will be ready, but I need some time to speak to her alone."

"Done."

It was 10:15 when Sammy called. At 11:20, Val appeared and by 11:45, Val had no questions left about the contract and asked for a pen. *What a beauty*, Dex thought, *but what was driving her, and what was her rush to jump into this relationship and what was the real deal with Carpozzi?*

Dex went out to the reception area and beckoned Sammy to come in to his office. Sammy signed without looking at the pages and motioned to Val to get up. She forced a smile, said thanks, and the two walked out as quickly as they appeared.

When Dex headed out of his office to talk to his receptionist, Don 'the Bomber' Carson who was rumored to be the next middleweight champion of the world was waiting in the reception area. He touched Dex's extended fist with his, hugged him, and followed the familiar path to the office.

"So champ, how's it goin' and you watching your weight?"

"Yes, sir. I am. How's the fight negotiations going? Have they come up with a better purse offer? I can kill that bum." Don threw several imaginary punches and finished with a right uppercut as if knocking out his next opponent.

"We're at $475,000 but I can nudge it to $600,000 if you agree to let him fight at a couple of pounds more. Does it matter to you if you give away two pounds? Does that make him stronger?"

"I could kill that bum at any weight. Make the fight, can I come into the ring last, I got Dondi-Z to rap for my entrance music?"

Twelve rounds where two guys who hit like bricks, slug it out till one is knocked senseless, and this dude is worried about who sings a rap tune? What a world, Dex thought. "Let me go through the numbers for you, champ."

"The purse is $600,000. Take off thirty-three and a third percent for your manager, another ten percent for your trainer, one percent for your cutman, taxes, and training camp expenses, and you end up with about $225,000, if you're lucky."

"What about your fee?"

"Deduct another $25,000."

21

"Okay, make the deal, but only if you get me six weeks to train and get the promoter to cover training camp expenses out of his share, and tell him I need an advance of $75,000 to hold me over."

The future champ was no fool and that's the way boxing deals are made. The Bomber smiled and started to leave, then he leaned back in the door and said, "Need eight good ringside tickets and two others, not near the eight, for a certain friend and get two extra airline tickets and rooms for five. What about concession sales, are we getting any of that?"

"I'll work the terms out, plus my two tickets and RFB from the casino," Dex said, referring to free room, food and beverages.

Dex thought a moment. "Don, I know you'll train hard. This is your big opportunity, so let me say this as a friend. I know you love women, if you keep your camp clean, you can beat this guy and the next fight is for a million plus and the title."

Don pumped his fist then hit his heart with a 'V' for victory sign.

Chapter Four

"God, I love this place," Dex said out loud as he jumped from the limo and into the large lobby of the Las Vegas Hilton and straight to the VIP registration room, where he was handed a glass of champagne. His thoughts immediately turned to Don and how he had done without drink or woman during the tough eight weeks of training. Now in the best shape of his fighting career, Don was ready, and a win in this fight would propel him to a sure seven-figure purse and championship bout.

"Mr. R., how nice to see you again. Guess you're here for the fight. Your suite is ready. Will you be needing two keys?" asked Patty, the beautiful and smiling hostess.

"One will be fine. I'm here alone."

"How's your wife and the kids?" Patty asked, not waiting for a reply as she called for Dex's bags to be sent up to his room. "There are a few bottles of Merlot in your suite and some chilled champagne."

"Thanks, and could you check on my dinner reservations when you get a chance?"

"Done, and if you need anything else, please call me."

Leaning back in the elevator and inserting a special coded key to be admitted to the high-roller floor, Dex caught his breath and looked again at the contract with HBO he had just negotiated for Don.

If Don won the fight the next night, he got a title shot and a guarantee of $1,750,000, and he was listed as an eight-to-five betting odds favorite at all the Las Vegas sports books.

Dex opened the door to his suite, walked to the bar in the living room, opened the merlot, sank into a soft chair and thought life was good. He called home, told Donna he had arrived safely, and was told the kids were good.

"Jamie scored the winning goal," Donna informed him.

"Oh damn. I missed the game, and promised Jamie I would be there." Dex felt guilty he had broken a promise to his family for clients, but this was a big, big fight and Jamie would understand.

"Love ya tons, and wish you were here. Gotta go to the pre-fight weigh-in. I'll call tonight. Tell the kids to watch on TV and maybe they'll see me in the crowd."

The pre-fight was a circus, a spectacle, a media event where two fighters got weighed in on a doctor's scale and were sometimes stripped to their underwear. Don was the first to be weighed. He was cut and chiseled, hitting the scales at the exact limit. His opponent was two pounds over the limit and although Don had agreed to that, the state boxing commissioner gave him one hour to knock off the extra pounds.

That was good news for Don because taking off the weight so quickly meant his opponent had to run it off or sweat it out, which could dehydrate and weaken a man.

"Let him sweat it off or run or go take a shit." Dex smiled to himself. Sun Tzu would have been pleased, the tactical war was going exactly as planned.

Don was in a great mood and loved the contract for the next fight, promising a win to make the team proud. Before he took a nap, he and his three sparing partners, manager and trainer went for a long walk. Dex had learned a long time ago boxers almost never went anywhere alone as there was always someone waiting to take a punch at him to prove how tough he was or at the least to claim the boxer had injured him and bring a lawsuit.

Dinner was to be chicken salad and lots of pasta to load Don with carbs, then another long walk. An old and wise trainer had once pointed out that long walks released the gases. "You don't want your fighter get hit in the stomach with gas, 'cause it hurts and smells up the ring," the old-timer had joked.

Dex had learned early on to keep his mouth shut and sit in the lobby with the old-timers and he learned just by being there: long walks after meals, hot showers the night before the weigh-in, Ex-lax if a fighter really needed to takeoff weight in a hurry, a small boxing ring if a fighter had good hands and strength, and a big ring with lots of loose ropes to bounce around if a fighter was more of a skilled boxer than puncher. Even the type of gloves was important. A pure puncher who hit hard would desire certain glove types which had a better chance of cutting the opponent, while other softer gloves favored a boxer, who could score points and not fear the damaging effect of getting hit by harder gloves on his skin.

"Hey, life is a learning curve and you can learn from anyone. There's always something to learn. It never ends," Dex would say to his students.

Dex was about to add to his learning curve, a new lesson, one he could not have imagined.

Chapter Five

Fight night in Vegas is electric. Dex could feel the excitement and tension in the crowd of 15,000 fans, some who actually liked the fights and followed the fighters and even knew their names.

Many were there to just follow the crowds, while others just stared at the celebrities lining the ringside seats. For many, the lust for excitement and hunger for blood was the gateway to betting. Others just showed they were 'the man', hitting the tables in the casino and betting at sums larger than they would ordinarily wager. The casinos knew this, and played to an individual's ego and desire to be recognized. High rollers were called by their initials, which made them feel good, and who didn't enjoy being pampered?

Casinos rely on the added excitement of fight nights and were willing to pay large site fees to promoters to hold the fights on their properties, and these fees were augmented by the networks and cable TV with their own payments to the promoters. Smart promoters, combining the site fee and TV money, were often ahead of the game before they even got a percentage of the ticket sales and concessions. That's the American way: those who took risks reaped the rewards.

This night was no exception, and as Dex made his way to his ringside seat wearing his favorite winning tie, he put his credential outside his suit jacket to let the world know he belonged. He wanted to be seen—let the people know he was a player. He often told his students the perception of power is power and the perception of money is money. *What was that great line by Shakespeare about the world being a stage and everyone in it a player or something like that,* Dex thought.

His seat at ringside, which he had earlier arranged with the promoter, was not accidentally right next to two pro bowl bound NFL football players who he quickly engaged in conversation. Dex also made sure he sat on the side of the ring where the managers and promoters sat, so he could get face time on national TV.

Yes, Donna and the boys would be watching, but so would the rest of the world back home. Many clients would see him, and there would possibly be some new ones, especially when at the end of the fight he would march into the ring victorious. All he needed was for Don to do what he trained to do—win.

Dex spoke to the blond-haired quarterback whom the world called Q and who sat next to him. He realized the HBO announcers were but 20 feet away and nudged the quarterback to stand and get some face time, knowing he would be standing next to him. People seeing this would think he was his lawyer and he knew his kids would love seeing their dad with their favorite ball player.

As Dex and his new friend moved forward, Dex froze, his stare fixing on an expensive suit and diamond cufflinks shaped like dice. Looking up Carpozzi, he gave a quick nod, a twisted smile and pointed a finger toward his right. Val sat next to him in a dark dress open to the navel, slightly leaning

28

forward and causing every man within eyesight to open his mouth and drool.

Mr. Quarterback looked at Val, then Dex who quickly recovered his composure and introduced the two. When Q heard Val was a client, the deal was sealed. Q became his best friend for the rest of the night.

Was the appearance of Carpozzi and Val a coincidence? What was going on? A thousand thoughts and questions flooded Dex's mind only broken by the loud roar of the crowd as the music of rapper Dondi-Z proceeded Don toward the apron of the ring.

"Here we go. This is it!" Dex screamed.

Everyone was on their feet, music blaring, people screaming, clapping. Then Mesirov, the opponent, entered the ring. Mesirov was not confident, thought Dex, who knew to follow a fighter's eyes for evidence of a hint of fear. The trainers had taught him the eyes gave away what a fighter was really feeling.

Every celebrity and every champ was announced as they climbed into the ring to applause. A color guard of military entered the ring carrying flags and next to them with microphone in hand, came Val who sang the National Anthem. The lady could hit and hold the long note, and the crowd went wild as she bowed to the audience. As Val finished, she quickly looked at Don and smiled.

"Nah, just my imagination, but why do I have that feeling in the pit of my stomach," Dex said to no one in particular. He elbowed his new friend Q and smiled, but it was an uneasy one. The fight was to begin.

The victory party was mobbed, young starlets wanting to be seen, athletes checking the women, promoters and managers huddled together, drinking, laughing as if they were best friends. Huddled at one corner were Carpozzi, Sammy, and a bunch of guys who Dex knew not to interrupt.

Q the quarterback and Val, who Dex was told was the sexiest woman at the party, danced the night away. Holding court at the center table was the victor, Mesirov, speaking in broken English about how he wore down Don in the later rounds two right-hand jabs set up the left hook. The thunder of a right-hand roundhouse that caught Don high on the temple sent him crashing to the canvas. Don crashed headfirst, and the fight ended just after the fight card lady had signaled the eleventh round.

All the news of the party, Dex learned secondhand since he accompanied Don to the emergency room of the Las Vegas Hospital where an MRI showed a slight concussion. A gash over his left eye required six stitches—really twelve since the surgeon knew to put six stitches in the cut and then six stitches to close the wound. He explained that would help healing without scar tissue forming over the eye lid. Scar tissue, is to be avoided for a boxer since in subsequent fights it becomes a target for opponents because it opens easily and bleeds, causing fights to end.

Dex didn't tell Don what an old-timer once told him that a rule of thumb was for each stitch, you had to wait 30 days to fight again to allow it to heal. Six stitches meant six months before Don could start sparring again—or was it twelve?

He couldn't remember but who really cared on this night? The glory that was to be was a broken dream.

The cab ride back was silent. Dex stared out the window at all the neon lights of the casinos, which seemed to be mocking him. Don cupped his head with both hands and it sounded as though he was sobbing.

"Listen, man, you did your best. You gave your all," Dex said, trying to comfort him. "It just seemed you ran out of steam in the ninth round, judges' score cards had it six to two in your favor after eight. What happened?"

Don stopped sobbing, looked up and said, "I let you down, my family, fans, friends, everyone and I gotta square myself with you, but promise me it stays between us." Dex nodded to show he wouldn't say anything. Don took a deep breath. "You remember the chick who sang the National Anthem? Well about three days ago at the public sparring session in the lobby where the fans hang out, she appears like a vision, piercing violet eyes and a great smile, not to mention a body that didn't stop. She shows up three days in a row, and I finally make my move on her and while giving her an autograph, she slips me her room key and a rolled-up note that she could really give me a massage and I should call."

Don stopped and looked off into space. "Her room was on my floor, and last night, I sneak into her unlocked room. She hands me a glass of champagne. I say I can't drink before a fight and she pours a little on her blouse and tells me to lick it off. She's unbelievable. Her blouse is open and her breasts are small but firm, her nipples are taut like hard erasers."

"What?" Dex exclaimed while trying to conceal how pissed he really was.

"You know, remember when you were a kid the pencils had hard firm erasers at the tip, well that's what she had, and

31

before I knew what I was doing, I exploded into her and she was like a demon, riding me and mounting me and like I don't know, a piston—never stopping. I came again and again and in an hour we were at it again. Three times, almost a forth, I slipped back into my room and the trainer who shared my room promised no one would know."

Heaven help me, Dex thought. Most boxers swore off all sex for three to four months before a fight because it made them mean and ornery, at least that's what the old-timers said. Nobody went three to four times a night and nobody he heard of ever drank before a title elimination fight and won.

"No problem, man. Your secret's safe with me— remember attorney-client privilege," Dex said as he tried to muster a smile.

I'm losing my mind. The whole world is getting ready for a fight except the fighter who's thinking not about the fight plan but about erasers, and taut ones at that. Even Sun Tzu wouldn't have an answer for this one. Why did I ever switch from corporate law?

After Don was safe asleep in his suite, Dex remembered he had given the casino very little action time and he needed to gamble to justify the free suite, gourmet meals and booze.

At 4:15 A.M. Dex made the cardinal mistake all casinos love their patrons to make: gamble when tired, upset or drunk, and Dex was all three and more.

Fully on tilt, he headed for a dice table knowing he would almost be giving his money away. Dex took a $2,500 marker he borrowed and signed a check, which if not repaid could be cashed by the casino, and in just under 15 minutes he had lost the chips and signed again for another $2,500, which he promptly lost betting with a buxom blonde in a low-cut dress who rubbed the dice on her left breast before rolling a seven-out. Enough for this night. He returned to his room and conked out as soon as his head hit the pillow.

He awoke the next morning, dressed quickly and took Carpozzi's white envelope with the 50 hundred-dollar bills down to the casino floor, moved to the cashier cage where markers were paid and handed the clerk the envelope, and in about ten minutes got back both markers stamped, PAID. Easy come, easier gone.

He hoped Donna had forgotten about the two-hundred-dollar bike Bret wanted, no how could he even think that after blowing the fee he got in about twenty-five minutes. He was pissed and Bret would get even a better bike but he felt no better, actually stupid. Gamblers hate to lose, even if the anger lasts only momentarily.

Turning to his left, Dex saw the expensive suit and diamond cufflinks of Carpozzi going into the private high-roller payout room. He stood there and in 10 minutes, Carpozzi appeared with a small attaché case. Carpozzi approached, "Sorry about your boy, seemed to have just run out of steam."

He then turned to Sammy and loud enough to be overheard said, "Got the $240,000 on the $150,000 we bet on Mesirov, 8 to 5 was a gift. He walked ten feet away to a slot machine where Val was seated, took her arm and the three headed for the exit.

During the flight home with Don, Dex felt he earned his fee and thought he now understood the term *blood money*.

Perhaps, he would give up on boxers and just represent promoters in the future.

Flying home, other events of that weekend were still unfolding. Darrell Scott, the real name of Q the quarterback, reached across the sheets to find his newest conquest was gone. He rolled over and felt for his shorts and smiled as his aching loins reminded him that last night was extraordinary. He loved his wife and adored his three young kids, but the road was the road.

The minute Q first saw Val at the fights and romanticized about them being together while she was singing, it was only a matter of the right time and place. That was the way it was with big and famous athletes. Early on, even at high school, the girls all wanted the quarterback, especially when he was blond, six-four and muscle on muscle. At college, even a couple of the teaching assistants were his for the asking, then the assistant dean came on to him.

Now in the NFL, the guys shared a silent code of never revealing what happened on the road, and in Vegas what went on in Vegas stayed there. Q and Val had chemistry from the first dance, and as she touched the back of his neck and leaned on him; he smiled and knew.

Somewhere between the fifth drink and forth dance, they exited the party and went to Val's suite. They were at each other's clothes while still in the foyer and naked by the entrance close to a couch, but Val insisted they go into her bedroom where a large white teddy bear was positioned on the table closest to the bed.

"What a cute little girl," Q thought, "she even brings her large white teddy bear to Vegas with her. Q knew when Val

34

saw his ripped and hard stomach, she would moan and reach out. He kissed her neck, and she slid under him and pressed her breasts and legs into his body. Lowering his face, he gently kissed her triangle, and she moved to accept his tongue. He was growing hard and she rolled over with surprising strength, mounted him and slowly began a rhythm of up and back. Soon he thought he would explode and take her like all the countless women before her.

She was different and while slowly heating his manhood till he screamed in ecstasy, she ever so gently took his large hands that could almost cover a football and tied them to the bedposts, then she took a blindfold and tied it over his eyes. This kind of thing never happened to him in Iowa or anywhere, and as she moved down with her tongue to his manhood and gently caressed him, Q felt something snap around his neck like a collar. Val untied his right hand so he could roll over on her and straddle her with only the teddy bear as a witness. She raised her right arm, holding the leash attached to the collar. He was pushing her hard into him, with each thrust he thought would rip her, but she kept moaning and pleading for more until he exploded and came down on her with all his weight. She lay there, smiled at her teddy bear and leaned back and kissed him like he had never experienced before.

The night was a series of contortions and positions and as the light began to shine, Q fell fast asleep. A man who had met his match and more. Val waited till she heard the snores, went to her teddy bear and unzipped the back, extracted a video camera, got dressed, left the room and went to a slot machine near the cage in the casino where she waited till summoned. What plays in Vegas stays in Vegas.

Chapter Six

Dex was so engrossed in his own thoughts he hardly noticed the smooth landing at Philadelphia International Airport till the passengers broke into applause for the pilot. He and Don deplaned and proceeded up the stairs and were greeted by Donna and the two boys who rushed to their dad. He placed the baseball hat from his head bearing the logo CARSON-MESIROV 2006 on Jamie's head as Jamie turned the bill of his new cap to the rear.

Dex hugged Brett and hinted that when they arrived home, he should go to the garage to see his birthday present.

Donna meanwhile, ever thinking and gracious, hugged Don and avoiding eye contact expressed her best attempt to say nothing, just feeling his hurt was enough. The two men briefly made eye contact, then touched fists gently, hugged, and said not a word. Dex, arm in arm with Donna, moved in one direction with the boys toward the baggage area while Don moved back to the large window overlooking the runway and stared at the plane. The reflected lights of the runway helped illuminate the pain in his face mirrored across the glass. "What a paradox. Life is sweet to be so cruel," he mumbled, turned, and walked out alone.

Arriving home, the boys ran to the garage where Donna on insistence from Dex had purchased a $350 mountain bike

Brett had coveted. The boys took turns riding in the woods near the house.

On entering the house, Pojo the golden retriever jumped on his master, ran in circles and expressed his love for Dex by chasing his tail. What could be better than home, wife, kids, and dog? He momentarily forgot the last several days.

After dinner and *Monday Night Football,* which featured a winning touchdown pass by that outstanding quarterback Darrell 'Q' Scott, Dex and Donna moved up to their bedroom and as he snuggled into her arms, he dozed and fell asleep. She kissed him softly on his forehead, pulled up the covers, smiled, and turned off the light. Life was good.

Returning to the office on Tuesday, Dex was greeted by the obligatory, 'Sorry, man', 'tough loss', and countless other indignities as lawyers, secretaries, and even Sara attempted to ease the defeat, but only made it worse. It's bad enough without an automatic expression of concern, when the sympathizer feels they should say something but doesn't know what to say or even worse, doesn't really care.

Five days away in Vegas, and now back at the office, there were many calls and e-mails to be answered. Soon he was deep in other client demands. "Yes, I do realize we haven't heard from any publishers but your manuscript was only sent two weeks ago. Give it a chance. A million books are sent out, and it takes time for people to read what we send. I did include the synopsis and the list of main characters." The caller's pain was evident in his voice and caused Dex to soften and add,

"Okay, let's talk in two weeks. Put it on your calendar to call me."

"Of course I care, but give the publisher a chance to read your material. He has scores of books."

"I'll call you if I hear anything first."

Acting as an agent was not easy, and getting someone to say yes was never a sure thing, so the ten or fifteen percent agents earned in commission was really well earned.

"No I'm sorry, but I didn't get a chance to hear your demo yet. I've been tied up out of town and hopefully by next week I'll have a chance to listen to your music. Call in about ten days." Calls kept coming.

"Yup, I reviewed the contract terms and wrote you and the company and e-mailed them my response, so let's give it a week or so. I don't want to call them because it shows we're anxious, and that's a sign of weakness. Listen, you have the talent and they will want you so play it cool. The price will go up."

The office was back to normal, whatever that meant to an entertainment lawyer and one call moved to another. At Sara's urging, she and Dex even had a quick lunch where most of the questions Sara asked were avoided, especially the ones about the fight and its outcome.

As the days went by Dex called Don often, but the boxer was getting more and more despondent. The cut over his eye prevented him from sparring, and there was nothing worse than being left to your own shame and guilt. Very few people were calling Don 'champ' anymore. Being ignored was the worst of all, especially since he had once tasted fame and glory. There were no press conferences, no reporters, no beautiful women loving him and he was no longer earning the large ring purses.

Everyone in the entertainment and sports world craves recognition and celebrity and all the fame that they bring. Is there someone who can't handle just a little more adulation? Each is looking to 'make it' have that hit, score that winning goal, go platinum, be adored and loved by the crowd. Few do achieve it and the worst of all is when they achieve it, to then lose what they have achieved. What's that famous poem? Dex mused. *Better to have loved and lost than to never have loved at all.* He laughed to himself. Try telling that to someone who had tasted fame, only to lose it.

Two weeks later, Dex attended the party for the National Academy of Recording Arts and Sciences, the group that does the Grammy Awards. It was always good to be seen at these parties and network with the 'in crowd' of the industry. When he spotted Val and Sammy, he casually worked into the flow and smiled hello. Val looked tired, but even so was beautiful and was holding court with Sammy close by her side. They were speaking to a couple of record producers, the guys responsible for coordinating the song, artist, and musicians and taking them into a recording studio, making magic happen and getting that great hit. Dex had learned record producers were celebrities in their own right. Without their unique blending of all of the components, the artist wouldn't record the tracks that sell records.

Dex shook Sam's hand, thinking how powerful his grip was, but not letting on his fingers were being squeezed together. *Why do guys do that? Must be a power trip,* Dex mused. *The more muscle in the hand the less in the brain.*

Val extended her hand and Dex thought momentarily of kissing it, then thought of Don and shook hands instead. They exchanged banal pleasantries before Sammy mumbled something, and they turned and were gone.

Dex sipped his merlot and felt stupid, like when years before at a dance, he worked up the courage, finally asked a girl to dance and she said, "No thank you," turned and left.

A musician waiting for his opportunity to speak to Dex jumped in and networking began anew.

"I write beats, and want to get the major labels interested in my music. I have two artists I want to sign to my production company. Can you help?"

"Call me at the office, and we'll set an appointment and we can talk it out," Dex said, handing the man a card. Dex, handed out about 15 cards that night. He had learned long ago the trick was not to hand out his cards, which could easily be tossed but to get the phone number of prospective clients, so he could contact them if they didn't make the first call. This was especially true of real athletes and stars who rather than offend at industry affairs took offered cards never intending to use them and tossed them as soon as they got the chance.

The real interest was expressed when the athlete gave his number and asked Dex to call. Dex had learned even this was sometimes just a way of politely getting rid of annoying pests by giving them wrong numbers.

Dex, even though on cruise control while handing out business cards and networking really had other questions on his mind. Where were Val and Sammy headed and why did they avoid him? What was Val's real story, he wondered as he

41

made one last sweep of the chatting crowd in case he missed anyone of interest.

During the quick sweep, that uneasy feeling in the pit of his stomach returned and he didn't know why, only that it was telling him all was not right in Tinsel Town.

Chapter Seven

The night air was chilly and Val shivered as she stood at the door of the limo while it pulled up. The driver quickly opened the rear door and she slid in, while Sammy moved to the front passenger seat next to the limo driver.

The sleek black limo moved into traffic, and 20 minutes later, headed across the Walt Whitman Bridge, leaving Philly and crossing to New Jersey where in another twenty-five minutes, it passed several large homes with manicured lawns. The neighborhood was stately and very expensive, and the limo eased to a large gated and private driveway. "It's Harry," the driver said to a little box on the gate, and the gate swung open. The limo proceeded about a quarter of a mile to an expansive circular drive in front of what looked like an old but maintained castle, turrets and all. Only the moat was missing to complete the picture.

The door opened and three men greeted Val and Sammy. Val moved down a long hall to a living room with steps to a large entertainment area where Vince Carpozzi stood to greet her. He was dressed in a black open sport shirt with pants to match, and he wore expensive alligator wing-tipped loafers.

"Good evening, my dear, and how did the night go? Did you meet any producers of value?"

"Not really. They all seem to be glib, but didn't have the experience or credentials we need."

"I spoke to some of my contacts and they recommended a couple of producers you should meet. I'll get them to call you and Sammy to set up a meet."

Val, thought for a moment and said, "What about calling Dex and get his thinking? He represents several well-known producers and one in particular who has a string of hit tunes he's written, and he's also produced a who's who of artists who have gone platinum."

"Yeah, what's it take, a million records sold to get one of them platinum records for the wall?"

"Dex has a pile of them on his office wall. Too bad he's still pissed about what occurred in Vegas."

"Sam and I saw him tonight, and he seemed polite enough, but he's hard to read—don't really know what he's thinking."

"Yeah, Don was his ticket to big-time boxing payoffs."

"I really think Don is his friend as well."

"Nothing a big fee won't cure. I'll call him in the morning and tell him it's time for you to sign with Can't Take It with You Records, to negotiate the deal on your behalf, and to make the contract fair and I'll give him a fat envelope. I owe you big time for the job you did on Don."

"Thanks, I felt bad for him."

"It wasn't personal, just business."

"And wait till I contact that big man quarterback and unload on him. He'll shake like jelly. He'll cave. Now, enough business, you look good enough to eat or maybe vice-versa." Carpozzi smiled down on Val who understood perfectly what was coming.

It was morning when the limo pulled up to her apartment and she got out.

The next morning, Dex was in his conference room with a young law associate and two aspiring directors who had written a script for a low-budget feature film. He was explaining the difficulty of acquiring funding that first-time directors and scriptwriters have.

"Talent is just a start. Businesspeople didn't get rich by just throwing money into projects. They need to see projections and ROI."

"ROI? What's that?"

The young associate eager to contribute and show he knew something replied, "Return on investment. Before one invests they want to know if it's safe, what they make on the deal."

The producers explained they had a load of friends and relatives anxious to invest.

"Yes, but if it's a large number of investors, the deal and structuring become more difficult, and there might be filing requirements with state or federal agencies or at least filing to get exempted. It's better if possible to have just a few investors, then you can save on time, accounting, and legal fees," Dex intoned.

"We could set up a limited partnership or LLC and protect the investors' potential liability only to the extent of what their original investment is," the young associate added. Dex explained that wealthy investors did not wish to have their entire wealth exposed in the event of a lawsuit and they preferred to limit their risk to only the amount of money they put into a project, and not one penny more.

Just then, the receptionist knocked on the door and poked her head in, excusing herself and asked if she could see Dex for just a moment in private.

"Excuse me, gentlemen, but proceed with the meeting. I'll only be a minute." Dex headed out of the room and closed the door behind, trying to hide his irritation. "Yes, what's so darn important?"

"That lady Val is here and insists on seeing you, and someone dropped this package off for you while you were in your meeting," she said, handing him the package.

"Thanks, but where is she?"

"Getting freshened up."

While waiting for Val's return, Dex opened the package and saw CTIWY RECORD AGREEMENT across the top of page one and about thirty-five typewritten pages. An envelope was also attached to the agreement with a check for $20,000 made payable to him and a message to review the agreement for Val and change whatever was unfair or objectionable.

Val returned, smiled that great smile of hers and extended her hand.

Dex, did an entertainment quick hug and peck on the cheek without really touching her so her makeup would not smear. Without a word, she followed him to the small private conference room adjacent to his office, sat down, and crossed her legs. "I'm really sorry but I really need your help and support."

Dex looked up and Val explained she was going to sign a record deal with Carpozzi who would help her get a producer and go into the studio, get her a hit record, promote it, and make her a star.

"Just that simple?" Dex asked.

"It takes a great deal of work, some luck thrown in and above all connections."

She smiled at that and she didn't need to answer.

Dex shifted his position, leaned forward then stood, moving to the window, looking out at what looked like little people on the street far below rushing off to do whatever little people rush to do.

"I've gone too far to stop now, and I want to be a star. Trust me I'm paying my dues in triple."

Dex wanted to say something about the Vegas dealings but held his tongue. "Give me a few days to review this agreement and make some changes, then we meet and go over the deal in detail so you know what it all means."

"Sure, but I'm signing no matter what." Val sighed. "Oh, and I really do appreciate your help and sorry for...well you know.'"

"Got to get back to the other meeting," Dex said and they parted.

The young associate, happy to be running a meeting without his boss, had moved to the head of the conference room table, and Dex motioned for him to stay put.

He remembered what it was like to be an associate under the thumb, even if a nice thumb, of a partner and perhaps that was why Dex years before split from his firm and went into practice on his own.

The key to being on his own was to have a book of business—clients paying you. Dex patted the $20,000 check in his breast pocket and smiled at the associate to continue running the meeting.

The next morning, Dex called his associate and Sara to bring their yellow pads and come into his office. "A record contract, if it is real, is the beginning of the jackpot. Most groups or singers will sign with a manager who can help them get signed to a label. It's something you seek and chase, and when the deal gets close, you need every line of the thirty-five pages checked. A few of the paragraphs give some rights to the artist and the rest of the contract language takes it back," Dex continued in almost a lecture-type voice to his associate and Sara seated across from his desk.

"I can't believe we're representing Val," Sara interrupted. A look from her boss instinctively caused her to shut up and listen.

"I want both of you to work together, and Monday morning, first thing give me your comments in letter-form addressed to Can't Take It with You Records, clarifying our position and what needs to be changed, and my guess is there better be at least 15 to 25 intelligent comments and explanations."

"I guess that kills my weekend plans," came a mumble from the other chair.

Ignoring the comment, Dex continued, "Artists know if they are ever going to get to the next level and get away from being a $250 a night bar performer, they need the clout of a record deal that gives them money, and most of all, promotion and distribution of their product. The company has to have the clout and ability to get that all-important radio airplay and TV exposure and get them known. How a record company gets their records played is another story for another day, but it ain't pretty and often crosses the line.

"Get working, and we meet Monday morning unless I call and then we'll hook up at my place on Sunday afternoon. That's it for now," he said.

It was good practice for them to rip the contract apart, and when he gave them his yellow stick-ums comments on Monday after they first presented their comments, they would then see what was important and what they missed. Besides, they could see something he overlooked and on this deal there had better be no mistakes.

He remembered the wise words of his sensei, "The teacher teaches the student, the student teaches the master and together they all learn from each other."

Saturday morning, Donna had gone to the hairdresser, the kids were wherever they were playing with friends, and Pojo lay near his master's feet happily dozing, while Dex, with two packs of stick-ums, was focusing on revisions to the contract. All his martial arts training really gave him an edge as he could focus for hours on end reading and revising without losing focus or being distracted till he finished.

That was the way he crammed for law school exams or even played poker, waiting to exploit weaknesses and mistakes of the other players when they got tired and careless. Sun Tzu would have been proud of this soldier. Wait for the right time and place to press, it's all about timing and placement. Cut off supply lines or get the enemy too extended, leave them weak and exposed, and then you strike.

Dex stopped for a moment and wondered aloud why the heck he was thinking of this as a military action or war.

49

Perhaps, his subconscious knew something he didn't realize. Pojo twitched, looked at his master and rolled back to sleep—he didn't have any problems.

There were many points to be covered in a record contract but the essence of the deal centered on producers, number of masters to be cut or recorded, song selection, cash advances to the artist, budgets to record the project, album releases, royalty rates, promotion and distribution.

One by one, Dex checked off the terms, making language changes and adding or deleting language that impacted his client. Several hours later, he smiled, stretched and was satisfied with his new-and-improved contract.

"Let's see what my associates come up with on Monday," Dex said as he patted Pojo who now did have a problem—he needed to be walked.

Chapter Eight

Monday morning, when Dex entered his office, on his chair was a seven-page letter with about 25 changes and comments to the record contract. Most of the comments reflected the typical writing of young lawyers who have a tendency to be detailed and dogmatic.

"Life is not all black and white, rather it's shades of gray. Compromise is the key to getting deals done," Dex would tell his students. "It's so much easier to simply phrase your comment as a question since the other side will usually know exactly what you're after, and this will frame the basis for negotiating. You understand what I'm saying?" he asked the two.

The two young associates eagerly reviewed the yellow stick-um marked-up contract, then revised the letter accordingly. Dex reviewed the revisions and he offered explanations for the various comments and changes he had proposed.

Sara especially liked the comment dealing with Dex's fee, in which he suggested that the record company who had advanced the $20,000 and who had added it to the recoupable balance owed by the artist would treat it as non-recoupable and non-returnable. The effect of which was that Val got a bonus or gift of the money, not having to ever repay the record company. Who ever said there was no Santa Claus?

He also requested tour support money so Val could travel without worrying she would lose money on her first set of gigs. When starting out, artists need to get exposure and experience playing before crowds but cannot command fees sufficient to cover all their touring expenses.

During the next three weeks, Carpozzi and the record company attorney went back and forth with Dex and eventually after some give and take, the deal was struck.

Dex met with Val two or three times to keep her up to date and they had even become friendlier, with the two going to dinner one night. All during this time, Sammy, her manager, was conspicuously absent, which was somewhat unusual for a manager since he should take a role in making sure the record contract would protect his artist. It became more and more apparent to Dex how Sammy was a Carpozzi foil.

During dinner, which was strictly business, Val after two or three drinks told Dex her life story, and what a story it was. She was raised in a little town in the south, dirt poor, and her older half-brother and one of his friends regularly used her as a play toy. She escaped at 17 when her dad's friend gave her a lift and put her up in his apartment. The friend had his own ideas of how she could make payment. Tiring, she also tried waitressing in LA for a time.

Val knew two things what men wanted, one which she became adept at doing and second that she had a natural gift, a beautiful voice with a raspy overtone, which with the way she looked was the complete package—almost. Why almost? She had no contacts, not knowing how to market her voice, and with almost no formal schooling, she decided to dance in a sleazy club rather than be a prostitute.

Carpozzi entered into her life. When he and a bunch of his pals saw her dance at the club during a lap dance, she learned who he was, and she knew he would be a meal ticket. What she did not know was what that meal ticket would require in return.

Carpozzi put her in an elegant apartment with a car, clothes, credit card and all she had to originally do was use the first of her gifts. The voice part came later, and she was given a voice and acting coach. The promise of becoming a recording star merely added to her loyalty and indebtedness.

Dex kind of softened toward her. She had it tough, and he was happy the contract was as good as it appeared, including an 'all in' record budget of $500,000, $100,000 of which was earmarked for Val as a non-returnable but recoupable advance meaning she only had to pay it back if and only if she earned enough royalties from record sales to cover the advance.

The dinner ended in a friendly hug as the valet pulled up Dex's car and the limo pulled up for Val.

Dex, as her limo pulled out, recalled some words he read by Napoleon, "Fame is fleeting, but obscurity is forever." Val was one lady who was determined not to be obscure.

The next couple of weeks at the law firm were normal—normal that is if one practices entertainment law. There was the NBA player who swore he never touched a drug but whose tests said otherwise. The chef who was writing a book about secret recipes, so secret he wanted the reader to guess at some of the ingredients. The composer who decided his

53

compositions should be in a movie but didn't write music, didn't play an instrument, and wanted to meet an A list director and hum him a tune. The really old lady who insisted on meeting Dex and telling him she was a songwriter of over a hundred tunes, but refused to let anyone see or hear them yet and wanted a publishing deal anyway. Dex got her a cup of tea and, when she was rested, gave her $20 to take a cab home.

Dex had learned entertainment lawyers had to be good listeners and have a certain sensitivity in dealing with creative personalities. Dex often said he had a very, very unusual practice, but none of his years of experience prepared him for what was to come.

Chapter Nine

Dex had two close friends, Jerry Hall whom he met in the first year of law school, and who had been one of the smartest in the class. He and Dex teamed together in a mock trial competition and did very well, finishing second at the nationals, an honor for them and the law school. Jerry, who was an academic but in a practical way, joined a large firm directly out of law school practicing criminal law, stayed for several years and when an opening for a constitutional law professor was advertised at a Midwest college town law school, he applied for the position.

Jerry sought out Dex to get his thoughts on the job, and at lunch was told, "You gotta do what makes you happy. Go with your heart, but what does your wife think?"

"She thinks it would be a great place to raise the kids and get away from the rat race—rather than fighting for two then three and maybe four windows in your office," Jerry said. Power and prestige in many large law firms is judged by the size and number of windows in your office.

"At my last firm for a while, I didn't have windows. I wonder where I was on the pecking order," Dex said, hoping to make light of the conversation and hoping Jerry didn't leave for his own selfish reasons. For years he had fantasized about starting his own firm with Jerry as his partner someday—Randle and Hall or Hall and Randle Attorneys at Law.

They spoke often and tried to get together with their wives at least once every year or two. The conversations were picked up in midsentence without missing a beat. Jerry had since advanced to full professor then assistant dean and was hopeful of becoming dean of the law school when the present and ailing dean stepped down.

The other best friend was Dex's earliest and first real client. Dex had met him at a recording convention when Will 'Trolly' Turner had no records, no released songs, and nothing happening for him. Dex, starting out on his own, had no real entertainment clientele. They were a perfect fit, and 20 years later still spoke two or three times a day.

Trolly was now one of the most prolific producers on the music scene. The songs in his publishing catalog numbered 250, and many had been used and sampled by some of the biggest names in the business. Platinum record recognition lined Trolly's home and recording studio.

Dex likewise had benefited from Trolly's success, and many in the industry felt it was a combination of talent by Trolly and legal and business ability by Dex, combined with over two decades of friendship that made them so successful.

Why the nickname Trolly? Rumor had it that he was born on a Philadelphia transit trolley while his mother was trying to get to the hospital and in appreciation for the trolley conductor's help, Will's nickname was Trolly and that's how everyone in the industry knew him and all respected his talent. If Trolly had one fault, it was his weakness for the opposite sex. He was charming, good looking in a clean sort of way, and though he had several loves, no one had managed to do that unmentionable word that was not in his vocabulary: *marriage.*

Dex and Trolly were on a real roll and the production deals kept pouring in with advances ranging from $20,000 to $35,000 a master, plus three to four points royalty on each record sold, plus a 'taste' of the writer and publishing share. A few platinum albums later, the new cars were being hosed down in his spacious garage. Actually, Dex would yell at his friend to save money and in the last two years, Trolly had become a real businessman, taking a keen interest in investments and enjoying his security and rising fame.

Though he understood the necessity of appointments, Trolly would occasionally stop by unannounced to see if Dex was available. "Yo, Trol, come on in. I've got a free hour, and we can catch some lunch."

"Love to, especially if you're paying, you know all artists and athletes get tremors in their hands when it comes to treating or picking up a check. Okay, but let's just go to the food court for a quick sandwich, I'm headed to my studio. I wanna finish P's single so it can be released before her CD gets ready to be promoted and she goes on tour. "

On the way back from lunch, Dex realized he hadn't heard much about what Val was up to, other than her being with Sammy testing various producers, and experimenting with some music demos. Word on the street was that she was unable to feel chemistry with people telling her how to sing and how to record her music.

Dex had been preoccupied with negotiating with a local TV station over the length of years and salary requirements of a weather lady who was being paid less than her male counterpart, and Dex was determined to right the wrong. Since the station really wanted this personality, this was the deal to do it. Supply and demand were often the determining factor in a negotiation. Who wants it more and shows it least.

It seemed stations with all their posturing about being individualistic were really following the lead of the highest rated station in the area. So when the leader hired a good-looking weather lady, the other stations followed the lead.

Dex believed there was a formula, as he told his associate, "By way of example, as we know most new sports anchors are ex-jocks and now suddenly the latest trend is that each station hires a mandatory blonde female to be part of the sports reporting team. When was the last time you remember a male evening anchor with a single hair misplaced?"

The VP of news programming had called back to tell Dex his numbers were too high and he wasn't in New York. Dex countered his weather lady could well be on a national network and maybe the VP was right and she should be in New York. "Give us a window at the end of the second year for 90 days to have the right to shop to network and we'll come down $15,000 in the second year, or give us a third year firm on your part at $50,000 more than you offered and we'll put this deal to rest."

"Let's talk tomorrow," countered the VP, who was having no part of a firm three-year deal at the proposed numbers.

"How about lunch at the Palm tomorrow and we can close this baby?" Dex suggested.

"Yeah, right, lunch at the Palm and you'll have three gossip column reporters in the next day's papers putting their spin and your side of the story that we were seen at the Palm. No thanks. I'll call you tomorrow if I get a chance."

Dex smiled to himself as if caught in a trap. He admired this VP. She was crafty and sharp, probably had read *The Art of War* when she was younger. "Great, tomorrow."

Class that week covered two assigned law cases explaining the subject of endorsements and sponsorships, and a law review article about marketing and branding of an athlete or entertainer to maximize his or her earning power. Dex had discovered no matter how inconvenient the time or no matter how tired he was when the lecture would first start, he truly loved teaching, and the interaction with his students invigorated him.

"Endorsements can be summed up in just four words, and you'll have the complete picture: Tiger Woods and Michael Jordan. What more do you need to know? A client like that and the millions they make from licensing their persona, the name, signature or likeness. This is an area you as young lawyers-to-be should think about." He paused with his back to the class and turned toward them. "How about Maria Sharapova, the women's tennis champ. She reportedly earns about $20 million just from endorsements."

"Professor, how do you really get clients in this field? It's so competitive," a third-year student from the last row in the class asked. Dex was always amazed how the last row in a classroom always filled up first, the theory being, the farther you were from the lectern, the least likely you would probably be called on in class.

59

Dex always made it a point to start the Socratic method of calling on students and questioning them, usually last row first.

"Not easy, especially when you first get out. I know if you think you can sit in an office and athletes or entertainers will call you, forget it. You will have to be out many nights at clubs and concerts, and travel to meet athletes all over the country because the competition is fierce. It's like anything else in life. If you want it badly enough, you just do it.

"Many of you would not like the chasing, but will prefer working in a firm that wants you to work on matters they already have in place and not being on the prowl for new business."

Dex momentarily thought of his own experiences. How many of his sons' school and sporting events did he miss while chasing down clients when he first started his practice? He hoped someday when they were older with kids of their own, they would understand.

Same with Donna, she understood his practice. What a champ. Dex made a mental note that her birthday was fast approaching and this time he was really going to get her something nice. He stopped thinking and continued.

"Okay, guys, next week, same time, same place, and have a great week. Next class we'll cover some of the new technology including iPods, the internet and video streaming and how they, in my opinion are killing the record industry." As always, a couple of students came up to the lectern with additional questions and Dex couldn't help but notice one student who was fiddling with his earbud as he probably listened to illegally downloaded music. Dex quipped, "Lucky for you, I mark final exams by anonymous numbers and not names."

Chapter Ten

The workweek was uneventful, and Dex enjoyed the weekend with his wife and the boys. Saturday morning there was a hockey game at the local rink. Watching the boys suit up in their gear was fun enough but sitting with other parents·and hollering and rooting for their team enabled him to forget everything else.

After the game, hot chocolate and pizza were in order as the boys hung with their friends.

"Can we go target shooting or go to the range?" inquired Brett, who even at his young age astounded the men at the range with his deadly accuracy.

"Maybe tomorrow. We've had enough today already."

Dex thought about going to the range but would have to go back to the house first, which was out of his way, to get their locked weapons and ammo. He pictured himself and the boys dressed in vests and bandoleers posing for a cover of the NRA magazine, which really would set Donna wild.

Donna had early on understood the boys were going to be involved in a variety of sports, but target practice was one of the adventures the father and sons shared. She did put her foot down when she heard the three plotting skydiving and didn't know if they were serious or just trying to get to her.

She shuttered when Dex who took the boys to the dojo to work out came home and they told their mom they had been allowed to throw knives and little stars at targets, and it was really neat.

Donna took it in stride, but turned pale when they told her, "Dad is going to let us work out with swords next time."

Life with Dex was like that. He was a fun-loving yet compassionate husband, and she learned to accept and even enjoy his adventurous spirit.

The evenings were Donna's to plan, and it usually meant if they didn't have to attend a social event for business, they had a relaxing dinner at a local BYOB restaurant, then arrive home early, relax and enjoy each other.

Sunday, when Dex returned from his tennis game, he showered, put on his football T-shirt and the foursome accompanied by Pojo settled in to watch the big game on TV. They rooted for the Eagles, but Dex was always listening for how his clients were doing. He hoped they won but didn't really care about the outcome. What was really important was that they played well, and above all else stayed healthy and were being paid on their contracts.

"Hey, Dad, did you just hear that? Your friend Q scored three touchdowns, two by passing and one on the ground. They won again. Can you get him to come to dinner sometime? Please, Dad."

Rather than dispel the notion Q was not really his friend and disappoint the boys, Dex responded by snapping, "Don't know. We'll see. Walk Pojo. He looks like he needs to go out."

Donna looked at her husband during the game and sensed all was not right, but she knew when Dex was ready he would speak to her about what was bothering him. A few hours later in his den and alone, Dex phoned his buddy Jerry. "Hey, how's the dean?"

"Not yet but you never know. What's hot back east, and congrats on the Eagles pulling that game out."

"Couple of new deals, nothing really exciting but remember that lady singer I told you about?"

"Not really, but what?"

"Well she's back, this time with a big recording contract, and I got a nice fee."

"Good for you, so what's the deal?"

"Too complicated, but remember that funny feeling I used to get in law school and then *bam* the professor would call on me and nail me to the wall. Well every time, she or one of her group calls, I get that same damn feeling."

"Go with your gut, bro, and what was the fee?"

"About $25,000 total so far, and I think it will go much higher."

"I should be so lucky. That's almost a fourth of what I make all year. Hey, how are the boys? Still target shooting with them? You really should be careful too many damn guns on the streets these days. They need to clean it up."

"Gotta go. Donna is calling for dinner. Stay well and talk to you soon. Don't be too hard on your students. Remember how we hated parts of law school?"

"Later."

Dex smiled as he hung up the phone. Life was so uncomplicated for his friend. He only had to worry about teaching his class, reading cases, and preparing final exams. "What a gig," Dex said, shaking his head.

Later that night, he and Donna watched *Boston Legal,* a lawyer show on TV where the young litigator and his older partner Denny Crane at the close of each show sipped scotch, smoked cigars and talked about life. They couldn't lose no matter what they did.

"Geez, if only it were that easy, but they didn't represent Val and Don and the multiple troubles they had."

"What do you mean?" Donna asked.

"Nothing."

Little did he realize he would soon be adding his best friend Trolly to that list.

Chapter Eleven

Dex and Trolly parked about a block from the restaurant and walked to the entrance of the Saloon, a fine Italian eatery located in South Philadelphia.

"Why are we here?" Trolly asked.

"I told you Carpozzi's guy called and asked if we could join him for dinner at seven tonight, and Trolly remember, none of your wise-ass jokes or remarks. This guy is serious. Don't piss him off."

"Who me? Forget about it," Trolly mumbled as Dex gave him one of those looks he saved for his kids when they would drive him near crazy.

The hostess directed them upstairs to a quiet little reserved area where seated with his back to the wall was the very immaculate well-dressed Mr. Carpozzi. On his left was Sammy, and next to Sammy was a heavy-set man with thick horn-rimmed glasses hanging on a cord nestled on the front of his nose. Seated next to Carpozzi was the beautiful and sexy Val, looking resplendent in a simple tight sweater set and black skirt. The pink sweater seemed to make her violet eyes even deeper.

"And you must be the famous Mr. Trolly, that writer who produces mega-hits," Carpozzi almost sang in a deep accented tone. Dex got a sick feeling in the pit of his stomach.

Trolly, unaware of the sarcasm, took the comment as a compliment and shook hands as introductions were made, only stooping to kiss Val's extended hand and sneak a short but furtive look at her tight sweater and all that it contained.

The man with the glasses was one of the top promoters in the country, probably the world. He had the power to get records played on the top radio stations everywhere, and Dex immediately recognized his name, Victor Pana of Pana-rama Promotions, Inc.

"I know you like Merlot, so try this. It's one of the finest, and Trolly, you don't drink so have a glass of this sparkling water."

Wonder what else he knows about us, Dex thought. *This guy really gets to me.*

"Food here is superb. You'll like the veal chop," he said, motioning to Dex with his manicured hand, "and Trolly, since you don't like meat, try the Dover sole with a side of broccoli."

Trolly, busy looking and speaking to Val, nodded.

"Dex tells me you can really sing, and I could really help you get a hit, if you would like to come over sometime," Trolly said to Val as Dex kicked him under the table.

Carpozzi smiled and took a sip of wine, saying nothing, but seeing everything.

Salad and then the main courses were served. Most of the small talk was done by Dex, Trolly, and Val with an occasional comment about the state of the record industry from Victor and how he thought it was getting harder and harder to get airplay, and that without airplay there was no such thing as a hit record.

Over coffee, profiteroles, and cordials, Carpozzi got to the point of the dinner meeting. "Sammy and Val think your man Trolly here can write and produce some hits for Val, so you get going, do that and Can't Take It with You Records will release the first single and six weeks later drop the album." Carpozzi glanced at Victor. "Victor here guarantees he can get the radio play, then we all make out. Right, Victor?"

"Yes, sir, that's the way it goes," Victor replied.

Trolly, obviously pleased with the prospect of working with the lady in the tight sweater suggested, "Val, in the next few days, come over to my studio so I can hear you sing, and we can work on some great songs you would feel right singing. You work out the terms with Dex and we can get started."

Not waiting for Trolly to even finish, Carpozzi turned to Sammy, nodded, and Sammy pulled a folded check from his breast pocket and handed it to Dex who looked down to see a 1 followed by five zeros and a notation on the memo line that read PRODUCTION FEE—THREE MASTERS.

Dex folded the check, and without a trace of emotion showing said, "Trolly gets three points royalty with bump-ups of one-half point on going gold and again on platinum."

Carpozzi nodded, "I don't want gold, only platinum, but you got yourself a deal." They all shook hands.

On the ride home, Trolly was already in love, and telling Dex that Val was one fine lady. Dex cautioned him, "This is business. Playing around with this crew of characters and Val could be trouble."

"Of course, but did you get a look at that body? Besides, she likes me already," Trolly told Dex for the zillionth time and smiled. "How does that man know so much about us? Did you realize the check was made out to Trolly Train Productions LLC?"

"Yeah, and he orders for us like we're kids, but he was right about what we eat."

"Who cares when I'm in love?" Trolly started singing hooks and melody lines to himself.

"A woman in a tight sweater is like a fine wine—not to be touched until it's time." Dex rolled his eyes and laughed at his friend. "What a crazy business."

Chapter Twelve

Trolly called the next morning and told Dex how much he had enjoyed the night before and asked if he had deposited the check. "I liked the way you handled the meeting last night, and don't forget to take your piece then send me the $90,000 balance. You can get that bracelet for Donna before you invest in the stock market. Keep that woman of yours happy. She deserves it."

"Thanks, and I'll take your advice. Here's some advice for you: don't mix business and pleasure on this one. Carpozzi is not to be messed with, and Sammy looks like a mountain, and I got a feeling he can back up his looks."

"No problemo, I got the message," Trolly said, "but she sure is fine looking, now if she can only sing."

"Gotta go. Talk to you later."

"Keep it to singing and let me know how the first session goes."

"Sings like a lark, but more powerful," Trolly said without even a hello, three days later on a call to Dex. "I mean she can really let loose. She has some set of pipes, and she has a raspy edge to her voice that really comes across, especially when I taught her to clear up her vocals and clip some of her long notes."

"Really? When did she come in?"

"Last night, and she came alone, spent the better part of four hours just singing and listening to what I had to say. She learns quick, and she can do several types of music. She writes pretty good but the lyrics are a little trite." Trolly paused for a breath. "I can really help her, and boy, would I like to really give it to her. Only kidding," he said before Dex could respond. "I was a gentleman for almost three of the four hours."

What Trolly omitted saying to his friend was that at one point when Val was back from the inner room where she was recording, she leaned over him while he played back her rough cuts and accidentally brushed against him. Trolly thought he was on fire. Pure electricity shot through his nerve endings.

"Val you do that again, and I can't be responsible for my hands."

Val smiled, gently put her face close to his and brushed her lips against his, then abruptly pulled away. She turned went back to the recording room and starting singing again.

Trolly forgot to turn on the controls and told her to try it again this time with more soul and emotion. Anymore emotion from her, and Trolly thought they could carry him out to his maker and he would be a happy man.

Making a hit record was no easy task. It took much time to find the right tune, one that fit the style of the singer. The song had to be one that mass audiences could relate to, and even more important, a hook people could remember. Then great rhythm tracks needed to be laid down, and each musician and his piece of work had to be carefully blended to make the right sound. The producer, with the help of an engineer, then must find the right combination of volume and mixing of the music before the singer even started to sing.

Often the singer needed to be coached, almost on each word or sentence, to sing the song the way the producer thought it should sound. Too often, a promising artist thought he or she could do it alone without the aid of a producer—kind of like a lawyer who represented himself and lost all objectivity.

Trolly was that rare breed of producer, artist, songwriter as well as teacher to bring out the best in the artist, and he was determined to bring it on home for this special lady who he was growing fonder of with each recording session.

Irony of irony, Val liked this charming man who was extremely talented and lived for his music and who just made her happy, even if she did not yet realize what was happening. She only knew that she felt at peace and secure when she was singing for him.

The search for the hit song was on, and many writers were approached and song after song was heard and rejected.

"We need a song that touches people and has a hook that everyone can remember from the first time someone hears it and can mouth the words," Trolly said. "When you hear it, the hairs on your neck will stand up and you'll know."

"And in the meantime?" Val said almost under her breath. "What about the timetable?"

"There is no meantime. We practice and rehearse, and practice, search, and rehearse."

"Okay, honey." The word slipped out before Val realized what was said, but not before the two made eye contact for what seemed like an eternity then turned away.

"I really like her, Dex I really do."

"Stop it. You really like anything that's not a man, and get off this sincerity bit. You're her producer, and that's it, nothing more."

"Okay, man, but she's something special."

"So is a snake before it strikes, and she comes with an assortment of rattlers. Do the friggin' tracks and let's move on."

Dex hung up but didn't like what he heard. Trolly was falling hard but at least he didn't have to go twelve rounds in the ring as Don had. Dex remembered he had not spoken to Don in a couple of weeks and made a mental note to call and see how he was doing.

Kid and clown as much as they did, both Dex and Trolly were all business when it came to their jobs. Dex had developed that ability to focus on a problem or negotiate a contract till he was satisfied the deal was complete or his client was protected.

Trolly, for all of his good nature, was much the same and a consummate professional who worked a song and the artist performing it till it was perfect in his ears and mind. Hence the search for just the right vehicle for Val to bring her performance to a peak was taking longer than expected.

Trolly was more and more enjoying the time together with Val, rehearsing and searching for the song.

He and Val would work in the studio, pouring over charts and lyrics as their coffee breaks together started going longer and longer. Sharing Chinese take-out was a favorite, and as they tried chopsticks and eating from little containers with wire handles, they learned of each other's likes, dislikes, hopes, and goals.

Dex understood what was happening and thought to himself. *Trolly, you can't see the forest for the trees.* That which to a casual observer would easily be discerned as possibly deep affection or even love, developing was just not said out loud or even to be discussed by either party. The emotions of the heart often override the powers of the brain without anyone being the wiser.

When two weeks stretched to three, Trolly was summoned to a little sandwich shop where he met with Sammy and Carpozzi.

"So tell me, Trolly, how's it going?" Carpozzi sipped his double espresso without even looking up.

"That lady can sing and we're looking for the perfect songs."

"We got a schedule to keep, and we want to release a single soon—real soon, like in two weeks—so I suggest you get your ass moving and stop with the chopsticks. You get my point?"

Trolly, unable to control his anger, stood and shouted, "Nobody—not you or anyone—tells me how to make music. You get my point?"

Sammy jumped to his feet but a wave of a manicured hand settled him down.

"Of course, Mr. Trolly, no one tells you how to make music. Good day."

Trolly turned to leave as Carpozzi sipped his coffee without another word said at the table.

"Maybe Mr. Trolly needs to learn some manners, Sammy, but not right now."

Chapter Thirteen

"We got it, we got it," Trolly shouted into the phone. "You gotta hear this song. I'm telling you it will make your hair stand on end. If you knew Val like I do, it's her life story and she feels every word. Listen to this." Trolly started singing into the phone, which he often did without regard to whether Dex had other calls, or whether there was a client in his office.

"The song is titled *Come In Out of the Rain*," Trolly exclaimed. "You don't know nothing 'bout Val, but she comes from a small and unhappy family background, lots of problems, was wild and a lost soul, and she finally found a man who understands her."

Yeah, I don't know nothing 'bout Val but decided not to say anything, Dex thought.

"Listen, we don't have all the words yet but..." The melodic and soft voice of Trolly began singing.

> *Come in, come in out of the rain*
> *You don't need to explain*
> *I know where you've been*
> *Runnin' wild, runnin' wild*
> *Take all the time you need*
> *To pull yourself through*
> *Cry it out, your heart's gone cold*

76

No need to explain
I'll ask nothing of you
Tomorrow will be better
Come in, come in out of the rain.

"It's sung as a love ballad, but here's the hook, we rap the chorus with beats. It's got everything."

Dex listened and smiled as he often did when Trolly sang but the song was brilliant, and the music combining a rapper with Val was really different. Rap, which was such a large seller of records, combined with a pop singer could unite and cross many audiences.

Often, when a producer lays down the music bed or tracks, it's done without the artist and when the rhythm is finished, that's when the artist comes in and puts down the singing. Usually, but not in this case as Val and Trolly were inseparable and worked each day and into the late hours of the night, rehearsing the musicians and doing the vocals with Trolly himself singing and doing the background vocals.

Val, by then, was as much a part of the production as Trolly, and with three different takes and some coaching, had put down the final cut that the musicians, Trolly and Val were all in agreement was the best. They only awaited the rapper to add the final element to the production.

The rapper they selected was Dondi-Z, the artist who had marched in with Don when he made his entrance at the Vegas fight when the crowd went wild.

Dondi-Z had been called by Trolly and as a special favor and for old times' sake agreed to add his prestige and value to

77

the project. A well-known name can bring additional sales to a recording, especially a name such as Dondi-Z.

The day he came to the studio, his chemistry with Val was amazing, and it didn't take long to record the song.

"Yo, man, this is bad. It's the bomb and will explode," Dondi said when he finished doing his take. "Hey, girl, maybe we can tour together on a couple of gigs if your record company puts the bread into the tour."

Val and Trolly both saw him to the door and as he left Dondi-Z quietly pulled his old friend aside and said, "Trol, you got to be careful, man. What you do is your business. I wouldn't mind a piece of that lady myself, but you're messing with fire, and it could burn your black ass. You got my drift?"

"Thanks for coming, man."

"They play tough, word on the street is they're connected. Rumor is they deal the heavy shit as well."

"Thanks, but it's not like that."

"See you, bro, and you get yourself another platinum record."

"Take care yourself."

"Whatever. Be careful. That lady is something special, and she can wail."

Trolly turned, pushed the volume knob on the soundboard, and the room was flooded with the sounds of *Come In Out of the Rain*.

Val touched his arm and placed her lips gently on his cheek, and they moved ever so slightly. Her mouth opened, and she was in his arms and being carried to the couch.

His hands, which were so deft and quick on the soundboard and capable of making great music explored her neck and caressed her breasts.

She moaned and slid her hand to the buttons on his shirt as he opened her blouse and touched his tongue to the delightful feast that hardened to his touch.

Her slender body melted to his, and he was surprised by the strength of her movements as she arched herself into him and raised her hips as she moved her hands to the zipper of his pants.

She was so beautiful he could hardly catch his breath. He exposed one breast, which was more exciting to him than if she were totally naked.

He entered her, trying to hold back, but she was moaning and moving up and down. The sounds to his trained ears were like a great chorus and aroused him even more.

Momentarily, he thought, *What do the French call it? The little death? The thousand deaths?* Oh hell, he couldn't remember but who cared?

Never before did he feel this way. As she reached climax, the grinding of their bodies tried to drain the last touch of delight as the sounds of their music provided the background. Val said something she had never before uttered, "I love you. I love you."

They lay in that wonderful world of serenity, where the world is at peace and all men are of good will. Touching, but not lusting, loving but not craving. Where everything is calm, and there is nothing but love.

This feeling was very new to both of them, and a bit frightening but for the first time they cared for someone else more than for themselves.

Many have learned to their regret that the romance and darkness of night conceals and covers many blemishes that are revealed in the bright glare of sunshine the following day. The lovers would be no exception.

Chapter Fourteen

A young third-year law student raised her hand and said, "Professor, you told me at the close of last class to save my question for this week, and what I wanted to know was how you go about representing athletes and football players in particular."

"Any reason why football players in particular?"

"Yes, my boyfriend is pretty good, and agents are starting to call him all the time."

"Well, it's a little involved, even if you have passed the bar and are a practicing attorney, a legal license is not enough to rep football players. Under the guidelines of the NFLPA—the National Football League Players Association—they are recognized as the exclusive collective bargaining unit. It's like a union, and they determine who can represent the players in the NFL."

"How do you get that?"

"You have to be certified, pass a test, pay a fee, undergo a security check supposedly for the protection of the players, and there are a bunch of regulations including being covered by insurance. So forth and more. If you need more info on how to register, see me after class and we can discuss it further. Now let's get into today's material if there are no further questions."

Another hand shot up. "Professor, what's with that heavyweight champ, I forget his name, coming out of retirement. He seems to be too old."

"Good question, and probably he's like so many retired athletes and even entertainers, once you have attained fame and fortune it's like in your blood. They really love the limelight and all it brings. They crave crowd attention, the camaraderie of those around them, especially teammates and the locker room. Your even forgetting his name proves the point. I had a client whose name I won't mention, but he retired while still at the top of his game, plenty of fame, money, good family, he had it all. Anyway, he calls me a year later even while working for a large corporation as a top salesman. Everyone wanted to meet him or have lunch or play golf, and the doors to the corporate world were always open to him. Tells me he wants to go back to playing ball and asked if I would arrange a tryout. I asked, why would you want to do it?"

Dex paused as the class almost in unison were leaning attentively forward. "And what the player said was rather profound. When a normal person dies he dies but once, when a ballplayer dies it's really the second time. 'What do you mean?' I asked him."

"Most ballplayers when they retire and are away from their teammates and the crowd go through feelings of withdrawal. In a weird way it's like they died. The new players mostly ignore them, and even the coaches say a hello and smile but they just get in the way. He said you had to live it to know what he was talking about. The players die but don't go to heaven."

The class was quiet and the hush was broken when Dex said, "Guys, we really got to get to the assigned material today."

On the ride home, Dex felt alive. It was a feeling that overtook him every time he finished teaching. It was a feeling of giving back.

Dinner at home was pretty normal that night. Brett was rushing to do some school project, which Donna was helping him with, and Jamie was as proud as he could be, having just learned he was to start with the varsity even though he was only a freshman.

"Dad, next week we have our first game on Monday afternoon, can you come?"

"Yes, you better believe I'll be at your game and cheering my head off," Dex said.

"Great, Dad, but please don't embarrass me by yelling your head off, okay? Please, Dad."

"Jamie, Mom and I are just so proud of you, but I'll be on my best behavior."

Donna yelled from the den, "Dear, don't forget to take out the garbage when you walk the dog."

Dex loved that even if he was well regarded, a known and hopefully respected attorney and professor, at home he was the dog and garbage taker-outer. Life with his crew kept him well grounded and gave him the proper perspective on life, his law practice, and family. He didn't get a chance to lose perspective when he was in charge of scooping after Pojo.

He reflected on the time he had been listed in Who's Who and when he came home and told Donna, she simply said, "That's nice, dear, but enough with the accolades and awards, it's what you believe and how you act that's important. Besides, Pojo needs to go out so please walk him."

What a far cry from most of his clients who dream of platinum records, MVP trophies, championship rings, and VIP passes, so they didn't have to wait or stand in line like the rest of the world. He remembered at the Grammys the bags of free gifts the presenters and performers received and how they complained about some of the free gifts not being worth a damn.

Who was to blame for the attitude of many celebrities? Dex thought he'd frame that question at the start of next week's class.

If a person was a superior athlete, everyone wanted to be their best friend. In high school, the cheerleaders loved the varsity athlete, and vied to date the stars. The teachers made allowances for homework not being turned in on time. When they got to college, it got worse. From the time they first arrived on the campus, life adjusted for athletes.

They lived in special dorms, ate at separate tables, had private tutors, and in many colleges besides the scholarship, books, and living quarters a special benefactor kept their palms greased with spending money. He thought back to one college campus he visited where six or seven Corvettes, all in the school's colors, were parked outside the football team's dorm.

Why then should the athletes think the laws apply to them? It was okay to speed just a little faster than the limit and go a little farther with a date and accept money from an agent or loyal alumni. It was okay on the most important fight of one's career to spend the prior night screwing and drinking your chances away because the rules didn't apply to them.

Trolly wasn't like that nor were a number of Dex's clients, but he made a mental note that with each new contract or accolade, regardless of cost to him each client would get this lecture and perhaps just perhaps, he could save them lots of heartache when they got older.

He decided to start with his sons.

Dex got up from his couch and went into his elder son's room. "Jamie, did you do your homework?"

Chapter Fifteen

The next couple of weeks were a whirlwind of activity. The master recordings had been delivered to Can't Take It with You Records, and it seemed the A & R guys—short for artist and repertoire, the ones who determine which of the songs is a hit, really liked the three cuts Trolly had produced.

The reality was Carpozzi made all the decisions but he relied on some of the people around him, especially the promotion men like Victor.

The key to any record becoming a hit was to get promotion, which really meant airplay. A record had to be played on the key radio stations in key cities, and that job was left to Victor and his team.

Promotion men spent years honing and cultivating relationships and visiting program directors at the various stations, trying to get them to put their artists' records on the air.

"Airplay is everything in making an artist big," Victor kept repeating to his team.

Sometimes the record gets light airplay, just a few spins per day or maybe medium. The best was heavy rotation, which meant the song was being played every hour so the listening public got it jammed down their throats till they remembered the song and being told it was a hit come to believe the hype.

The real question was, with all the records coming to market, how did a program director with only so much listening time on a station choose the songs to be played, and which ones didn't get airplay and became destined for failure?

Enter the promotion man with personal relationships who convinced the PD, short for program director to play his song. The real question is whether the best songs are picked, or is it something else?

Carpozzi, Sammy, Victor, and three other men who Victor brought to the meeting sat in the office of Can't Take It with You and discussed the marketing and promotion plan for Val's record. It seemed simple enough: break the single in several key markets on key stations and the record was on its way.

Carpozzi pecked away on his computer and said, "I'll take New York and Washington. I can deal with some people I know, perhaps an envelope and a couple of cartons of records delivered to the back door of the PD, so when the CD comes out, he can sell them to some stores he knows for extra cash."

"The artist won't know the real sales figures anyway," Victor said.

"Your territory is Boston, and you have allocated $25,000 in cash to get us medium to heavy rotation and a couple of interviews on air." Carpozzi pointed to a stocky man sipping some bourbon and water.

Carpozzi interrupted, "Get me Philly and LA. What will that cost?"

87

"Let's break it on the east coast first then the west coast," Victor replied.

"The guy I need to see has a couple of markers from gambling in Atlantic City, so if we can get them canceled or paid off, he'd be most grateful."

"Done," Carpozzi replied.

One of the other men said, "Is Val available to visit a few cities? We can arrange TV exposure on a couple of talk shows and a few record stores." Victor answered without looking up.

"Too early for in-store visits. Let's wait till the CD drops, but I like the idea of some TV appearances."

"Who do you know?"

"A friend has a loan application for a new business venture of a VP of operations at a major network, and I'm sure if the loan is approved, the VP would repay the favor. I'll get working on it," said the man slouched on the couch.

"How much?" Carpozzi asked.

"I can get it done for a weekend in Vegas with a couple of hookers thrown in for the loan officer."

"I love capitalism, and the free market system." said Carpozzi, smiling.

The men raised and clinked their glasses in the air, and they laughed. Then, with a motion of Carpozzi's arm, they were asked to exit the room.

"Sammy, hold up a minute." Carpozzi looked at his childhood friend and waited another minute till the room was clear.

"So what do you hear?"

"What do you mean, boss?"

"About that Trolly jerk and Val?"

Sammy had a puzzled look on his face and didn't reply.

"Keep an eye on them, and you go with her on the trips. She doesn't seem right, and I want to keep her in play."

Sammy didn't quite understand his boss about keeping her in play but he welcomed dealing with the situation when the right time came. His anger was growing at even the thought of Trolly together with Val.

Chapter Sixteen

The making of a hit record, in some ways was similar to the planning of a military action, requiring advanced preparation, assaults on an objective, surprise moves, massing of troops or supplies, and when it was needed, adding new and improved weapons with which you gained and achieved the desired result.

In this case, the new and surprise weapons were money and fear, which when properly positioned caused a number of individuals either bought with their own greed or fear of not complying with the requests of the promotion men to play the record. Sometimes the action was covert, other times the military action to get the record played was more overt.

"So you got to hear this record. It will blow your mind. Val sings her ass off, and we'd really appreciate your putting it into rotation." He slid a box of chocolates with a picture of Val tied with a ribbon to the PD. Just as in Forrest Gump you never know what's inside. The PD found a tight roll of fifties sitting next to the chocolate-covered cherries.

That night *Come In Out of the Rain* was played over and over in Boston.

Atlanta was a tougher problem as the PD of the major station didn't care for the song and was gently persuaded he should play it when his favorite car parked in his reserved spot was vandalized, with key scratches from the front fender to the rear door. The very next night, three tires were slashed and a promo picture card of Val Clifton and her hit single was found near the last remaining good tire. The single became a big hit in Atlanta within two weeks.

The following week Jerry Peters, a VP of a large network, was called into Third State Regional Bank and pleasantly surprised when his loan application to start a series of car-washing franchises was approved without his personal guarantee.

He whistled to himself as he patted the bank check for $750,000. Val appeared on two national talk shows on his network and sang her hit new song. The hosts even raved and predicted she would go platinum.

Philadelphia followed suit and a disc jockey who could make or break a new record just carried on about the beautiful girl with the raspy voice and 'the slammin' production' of Trolly. What a hot combination they were and listeners should be on the lookout for the CD, which would be out in about three weeks.

When he hit Atlantic City, the disc jockey was called into a casino host's office and told he didn't owe the casino two markers for previous gambling debts. He was so drunk the last visit, he forgot he paid them off before he left. He was not as surprised in his comped suite to find a stash of white powder taped under the wash basin.

The wonderful thing about the record industry, once the big stations started playing the hit, smaller stations followed suit. The stations played popular and recognized songs, so listeners would stay tuned to that station. This way, they maintained ratings, which was how advertising rates were determined—the higher the ratings, the greater the advertising revenues.

As the record started to garner more airplay, Can't Take It with You was doing its part, and the single was starting to sell not only in the traditional way but also on the Internet, and the song could even be purchased as a ringtone for cell phone use.

Val and Sammy went on the road, visiting several radio stations, walking through, chatting and posing for pictures with the staffs. They also always took the time to meet and greet the PD and the main jocks, even going to dinner or partying with them.

Sammy and one of his assistants were always nearby, and from time to time handed small packets of powder to one of the partygoers who would disappear for a few minutes then reappear much livelier.

When Val got a free moment she would grab her cell phone and walk away from everyone to call Trolly.

"How are you? Yes of course, I miss and love you. No, it's hectic and we go from one station to the next but I'm excited the single is really starting to take off and I'm told next week in Billboard Magazine it hits the charts at #22 with a bullet. I do miss you and wish I was home, no he doesn't bother me but I get the feeling he watches me like a hawk."

"Be careful and when you get back we gotta do something about…"

Val cut him off in mid-sentence, "Sweetheart we got to be careful just a little bit longer, got to go Sammy is looking around. Kiss, kiss."

Trolly sat back thinking about Val and reached for the phone and called Dex. "Yo, how you doing?"

"Fine. You okay? It's 1:30 in the morning."

"Want to get a drink or breakfast?"

"What's the deal? You don't drink, and it's kinda early for breakfast, but come on over and I'll put up some coffee, but you don't drink that either."

"On my way."

Dex knew this would be a long night, and it wasn't the first nightly visit, so he was prepared to hear his friend tell him he really liked Val—or was it love—and so on and so forth, blah blah blah. When Trolly settled in with a glass of water and with tears in his eyes spoke of love and wanting Val to move in with him, the severity of the situation caused Dex real concern.

He understood that his buddy was treading into deep waters, and this was not the crew to upset. Soon Trolly would be in over his head.

"You love women, period, and this will pass. Remember when you fell in love with that—"

Trolly cut him off. "Stop it. This is no joke, and I didn't come over here at two in the morning to kid around. What are we going to do?"

Dex for a second wanted to reply, "What do you mean we? It's you," but decided Trolly would not appreciate any humor.

"Let's find a solution, but it can wait till tomorrow. Let me sleep on it."

Dex pushed him toward the door, hugged him good night, and headed back to his den and a glass of Merlot. It was going to be one of those long nights. Dex often said, "The true definition of friendship is when you call someone in the middle of the night and say you need help burying the body and they reply 'When and where?'" How many friends would do that for you? Dex knew Trolly would and he couldn't let him down.

Chapter Seventeen

Vince Carpozzi called out to his secretary, "Get me Alex over at World International Talent Agency on the phone and tell his horn-rimmed assistant when he answers to put me through or he'll think he really is an owl when I get done."

A few seconds later, he was on the line.

"Mr. Carpozzi, it's an honor, and how are you, sir?" Alex said.

"Fine, Alex. How goes it?"

"Couldn't be better. Record industry is really changing, but thank heaven groups are still touring, even if not as frequently. The ticket prices go up and up and the public keeps paying."

"Glad to hear it. That's why I called. I need a little favor."

"Name it, and you got it anything within my power."

"I hear you got a mini-tour going out in two weeks with two groups, and I'd appreciate you adding Val Clifton to the tour. You can even let her be the third act and sing two or three songs to open the show. I don't need anything elaborate. I just want to get her exposure."

"Mr. C, I'd love to help but can't do. The manager of The Slippery Rocks has contractual say over any acts joining the tour."

Alex almost stopped speaking as he realized he just committed two mistakes, the first calling Mr. Carpozzi 'Mr. C' and the second saying no to him. He waited for the blast that was to come.

"That's unfortunate. Perhaps you could speak to that manager or cancel the tour or tell him I'd look kindly for the favor and he might need a return favor one day."

"Let me make the call, and I'll get to you, sir, by no later than tomorrow, if that's okay."

"Sure, Alex, and thanks for your concern. My very best to the wife and your two lovely daughters. I understand they are adorable. They go to that fancy private school near the park, don't they?"

"Listen, Max, a third act will just add to the attendance, and she's really hot. Her single is zooming up the charts and you don't have to pay her anything or reduce your price. I'll cover her expense."

"Screw that. I don't need no third act, and I don't give one flying whatever what record company she's with."

"Max man, be reasonable. I need this, and you got to agree and I'll make it up to you. You never know, you might have an act you want to sign to Can't Take It with You someday."

"Fat chance in hell. What's he got on you anyway?"

Alex didn't respond.

"Okay, but her credits and signage are fifty percent of my acts. She gets 20 minutes, no more. She's no headliner and I'm not making her no star."

"You're the best, and I won't forget this. Take care."

"Mr. Carpozzi sir, this is Alex. It's done and your artist will be touring. Who can I speak to regarding the logistics and her backstage requirements?"

"I'll have her manager Sammy contact you, and Alex thanks. I remember favors. If you and the Mrs. would like to use my villa in Paradise Island next weekend, there will be two airline tickets in your name waiting on Friday and a limo will pick you up when you land. No, make it four tickets and take your family."

"Sammy."

"Yes, boss?"

"Get a hold of Val. I want her at my place at 8:30 tonight, and I'll give her the good news."

"Pick her up."

"Yes love, of course I'm happy to be back, and tonight is great."

Val tossed her hair and anticipated spending the evening with Trolly who she really did miss. It had been several weeks, and though they spent long hours on the phone, she ached to be touched and loved by him. She smoothed her dress and nodded approvingly at her sleek figure and her hair, which now was in long rows of curls which seemed to fit the new Val.

"Hold on a sec. The other phone is ringing. I better get it."

"Hi, Sam…Eight-thirty? We just got back, and I'm exhausted. Can't it wait till tomorrow…? No you're right, of course I'll be ready at eight, and I won't be late."

"Trol, it's Sammy on the line, and he scheduled an interview and dinner," Val lied.

"No, this has got to stop. I need to see you," Trolly said.

"Dear, what can I do? Just as soon as it's over I'll call and we can get together late. I love you. Gotta go."

Sammy and the limo arrived at 7:45, and he called up to Val.

"Just a minute and I'll be down," she said as she touched the curling iron to her hair, took a quick look in the mirror, grabbed her coat and pocketbook.

The ride was almost in silence, with Sammy staring out the window and Val hoping this would be a brief meeting and feeling a little nervous. It was almost as if she were betraying Trolly, and she was upset she lied to him. It was for the better.

They arrived at the gate, were admitted to the grand entrance, and Sammy left her in the long hall. She was summoned up the circular staircase down the hall to Carpozzi's master suite and bedroom.

Dressed in a silk lounging jacket and casual trousers, Carpozzi was seated in front of his computer when she entered the room.

"Good evening, my dear. How's the star? The record is climbing the charts every day. What would you like to drink?"

He rose, walked over to her, gently kissed her, and handed her a glass of chilled champagne. "Sit here next to me," he said as he sat on a lounging couch near a wide-screen TV, which was playing the new video of Val singing her hit single.

"Let me take your coat."

"I'm kind of chilly, and I'll keep it on."

"Nonsense." He undraped the coat and looked approvingly at Val. "I like the new hairdo. It fits you, and now for some exciting news. You are going on tour in two weeks, playing on a bill with the Slippery Rocks, which means you'll be in front of 10,000 people a night and getting a load of press and exposure.

"Plans are already being made for your band, which means tomorrow you go into rehearsal, and Sammy is lining up a road manager, and it's all set in motion."

"That's great. It's just I'm tired from the publicity tour and don't really feel so good tonight. I may even have a slight temperature." Val took a sip, already knowing what was coming next.

Carpozzi put his hand on her forehead. "You don't feel hot, but maybe this will help," he said, handing her a gift-wrapped package.

As she tore the paper and removed the ribbon, his hand slid to her throat and gently massaged her. The velvet box was oblong, and when she opened it there was a gold-and-diamond necklace with a diamond-studded record locket engraved with COME IN OUT OF THE RAIN.

"It's beautiful. Thank you."

She moved to give him a hug, but that was not the message or thanks he wanted.

"Let me put it on you," he said, closing the clasp around her neck. He kissed and turned her around, then led her to the bed and slowly undressed her.

What seemed like hours later she checked and he was fast asleep as she got her cell phone and closed the bathroom door.

"Trolly," she whispered, "the interview went late and we had to go to dinner with some guy and his date. Love you and see you tomorrow." Not waiting for a response, she closed her cell phone.

Carpozzi called her name.

"A girl has to go to the bathroom sometime," she said as she slid under the silk sheet next to his naked body. Carpozzi was turned on his side and didn't notice the tears welling in Val's eyes.

Chapter Eighteen

Dex momentarily surveyed his class when he noticed the raised hand. "Professor Randle, I invited my boyfriend to class today if it's okay with you. He's the one I told you about who plays football."

"Sure, I know who he is. Trent, nice to meet you, and take a seat next to your lady. You can ask questions, but no side talking during class."

"Yes, sir. It's nice to meet you, and Sonia speaks highly about you. She really enjoys your course."

"So before we start class, any questions about what's happened since last week?"

Sonia's hand shot up, and she asked about agents and how you pick one, looking at Trent as she spoke.

"There are a number of very competent agents—actually they are really contract advisors but the newspapers call us agents and others have called us a number of things, some not so nice," Dex said as the class laughed.

"The trick is to get someone who has a track record, is honest, and cares about what he or she is doing. Yes, Sonia, there are a number of women who are agents and very good at what they do." Dex paused and looked directly at Sonia and continued. "They should have knowledge of the teams, how they negotiate, what they need, knowledge of the salary cap, and also understand give-and-take in doing a deal.

"The commission is pretty much set by the NFLPA and is three percent, and you should not pay more. Financial planning, what you do with the money you get is of course very important and financial advisors are also regulated. Bluntly, you need to be careful and not go with the first agent who offers you a car or money under the table as it can ruin your career."

Sonia looked at her boyfriend and nodded.

Class ended with Trent thanking Dex, and he and Sonia walked out hand in hand.

Dex thought they were a nice couple and wondered how long they would last when Trent Prichard got the big money and hit the road with all the temptations it offered. He hoped Trent would be different and survive the fame and ego that affected so many big-time athletes.

The next few weeks were uneventful. Val was on the road touring, her full CD had been released and was moving up the charts. Airplay was plentiful and Can't Take It with You Records threw a record release party with a who's who of the record industry.

Many industry executives, promotion people, disc jockeys, athletes, and nubile attractive models mingled, ate, and drank while awaiting the appearance of the rising star.

Trolly was there trying not to look at Val, and Dex had brought his wife, Donna, who usually preferred to stay at home with the kids but he insisted she attend.

"Dex, nice to see you, and this must be the lovely Mrs. Randle," Vince Carpozzi spoke as he kissed Donna's hand.

"Nice to meet you. It's a wonderful party, and thank you for inviting me," Donna said.

"Please enjoy yourself, and let me get you a glass of champagne. Your husband is a very good attorney, and you must be very proud of him."

"He's an even better person and father," Donna replied and wanted to kick herself for even discussing Dex with him. She instinctively felt this man was evil...sinister and should not discuss her family with him.

Dex intervened and took his wife by the hand and moved toward Val.

Both women looked at each other, and Val extended her hand and thanked Donna for coming.

"You're very talented, and best of luck with your tour. I'm sure you must be very proud and excited and only good things should come to you."

"Thank you, and you're everything Dex and Trolly say about you and even more." Donna immediately liked her. Though not taken in by her statement, she felt Val was basically shy under her protective façade and under the right circumstances could have been sweet.

Val took Donna by the arm and asked if she would like to go to the ladies' room to freshen up. Off they went as if two schoolgirl chums who had known each other for years.

"I love your jacket. Where did you get it?" Val asked, trying to make light conversation.

"Oh, I've had it forever. How's the tour going? They can be very grueling."

"You're right. Donna, can I ask you something? I know you, Dex, and Trol have been close friends for years and he trusts you guys with everything. Has he said anything about me? I mean—"

Donna cut her off, "Trolly can't think about anything but you, and he drives Dex nuts about making a life with you."

"If you only understood. What am I to do? I'm so entangled and messed up I could kill myself or run away, but I could never escape from Carpozzi. He'd find me the world over and…"

Two pretty playthings entered the bathroom, and Val stopped short as the models compared their dresses and who were the lucky guys they were going to have and take them home.

"I'm going home with that movie producer and by the time I'm done with him, I'll be a leading lady."

"Leading, you might be, but a lady, never." both models laughed and headed for the exit.

Donna approached her husband and quietly asked if it were time to go home yet.

Dex had not yet worked the crowd, and there were too many potential contacts to pass up the opportunity.

"Just give it a few more minutes. I need to talk to a couple of the guys, then we can leave."

"Dear, who's that huge guy in the corner who keeps staring at Val?"

"Oh, that's Lethal. His real name's Sammy and he works for Carpozzi and acts as Val's manager. Why?"

"He gives me the creeps and looks like he'd rip the wings off a bird for the fun of it."

"Nah, he does as Carpozzi orders." Dex marveled at his wife's accurate intuition and at the same time he got that damned sick feeling in his stomach.

"I feel sorry for Val. She seems so nice but lonely. She really likes Trolly."

"She's not that sweet, and she can handle herself pretty well, so don't be so concerned."

Dex had not really spoken to Trolly about the Val situation since the night Trolly came over and though they spoke at least twice every day neither had broached the subject, preferring to let it just exist but not be faced. Dex felt that sometimes in life, not dealing with something is actually doing something or else it certainly sounded as if that made sense. Neither man wanted to go where tough decisions had to be made.

The car ride home was quiet. Dex, in his mind, was trying to come up with an orderly solution to a jumbled mess while Donna thought about what she had to get ready for Brett and Jamie the next morning.

Her thoughts turned to Val, who she felt very sorry for, despite the glamorous life she was leading. No good was going to come of this triangle, it was almost like a Greek tragedy unfolding before her very eyes. This was no play.

Chapter Nineteen

Sara buzzed Dex and told him, "One of your students is on the line with a Trent Prichard, and they wish to speak with you."

"Really? Put them through."

"Sonia, hello. How are you guys? Trent, if you come to one more class, you'll have to take the exam," Dex joked.

"Professor, could I come in to see you?"

"So many agents are calling at all hours of the day and night, even chasing my parents, and I don't know which way to turn."

"Sure, if I can help."

"One said he'd help my dad get a job and he could help out in the meantime, and my parents could sure use some money."

"Look, you still have two games to go, and probably your team will be going to post-season play and you don't want to do anything to mess up your eligibility and affect your school and your credibility."

"Please just give me some pointers on what I should do or not. I really liked listening to you, and we both get good vibes."

"Okay. Tomorrow at 2:30, is that good for you?"

"We'll both be at your office, and thanks."

"Understand I can only give you general advice, and since I'm also registered with the NFLPA, this meeting is not about hiring me as your agent."

Trent's story was not unique. Born to parents who were working to provide for his brother and sisters, they were just getting by. Trent's dad was a bus driver who was out on disability and his mother was on a low hourly rate job. Trent was the first to go to college.

He was blessed with great speed, able to run the forty-yard dash in 4.45 seconds, and also possessing power. It was evident from an early age he would become an exceptional athlete.

He was a high school All-American on a state championship team, several college coaches came calling, and he was able to go to college on a full scholarship with room and board.

He told Dex of one coach who promised his parents to look after him as if he were his own. He would get a great education and a college degree, the coach promised.

Trent laughed as he continued, "I'm in my fifth year because an injury was going to sideline me for the season so they red-shirted me, which gave me an extra year of eligibility, and I'm still five courses short of my degree, but I should be a millionaire by this time next year."

Like so many scholarship athletes he, as his fame on the field evolved, was sought after by young women—students wanting to befriend him and those who sought to profit by exploiting him.

One agent in particular had approached his parents, offered them a beautiful house and spending money to use so they could escape from their neighborhood till a contract could be negotiated with a sizable signing bonus.

Trent had another agent tell him one particular team would draft him in the first round or no lower than high in the second, and since he was close friends with the coach, he would then make sure Trent would be set for life.

"Enough of this," Dex said. "Let me set you straight. No agent can guarantee a team will take you because they like that agent. It's against NCAA policy to hire an agent when you still have games remaining to be played and you can't take money or anything of value nor can your parents accept things of value.

"Just be cool and finish the season and the bowl game and there will be time enough to hire a representative. In fact, your school has a panel of professors and experts who can screen the agents and help you choose the right one."

Trent looked at Dex and said, "Professor, could you help me pick the right agent and be my lawyer?"

"Let's wait till the season ends, and of course you're welcome to attend my class.

"I don't want to sound cheap but I can't even take you two to lunch and pick up the tab or we'd violate some rule or another."

They both laughed and left his office.

I sure would like to help Trent, and I would love to represent him when the season ended, Dex thought as he watched them head for the elevator.

On the other side of town, another game was about to be played.

Carpozzi called in both Sammy and a thin nattily dressed man to his office, and once seated, he closed the door and put on a tape, which they watched, riveted to the large TV screen. Sammy whistled as he saw Val in action as a hunger welled up deep in him. The thin man turned to his boss who spoke.

"Here's the deal: we send a copy of this to Scott and invite a meeting. His team is hot, and Monday night they play a low scoring team. You suggest to Q that he keep the score down. Tell him they can win the game but not score enough points to cover the spread." Carpozzi smiled and said, "My associates and I bet on the game and we make a bundle. I'm told the spread will be six points, and he must go under. He'll take one look at the tape with him doggie style and with the collar, and he will do anything for his wife not to get a copy of that video."

Sammy laughed. "He'll probably wet himself before he completes a pass."

"Boss, you want I should meet him in person or over the phone?"

"You dope, over the phone, and send the tape as a training video but mark it personal and confidential on the outside of the package. Better yet deliver it to the player's PR office, and they will see to it that he gets it. Get a prepaid cell phone and give him the number to call at a designated time without fail. After the contact, destroy and get rid of the phone. Got it?"

"You got it, boss."

"Make sure he understands if he screws up, the tape goes to his wife for her and his kids to watch."

Sammy moved in his chair. "What about Val? It could destroy her career."

"Look carefully and you'll see her face is mostly covered and we air brushed her features out. Besides, he's not letting that tape go public."

"That's Val? I didn't recognize her," said the thin man.

"Forget you heard that, and never repeat it. Understood?"

"Yep, boss. I already forgot."

Sammy and the thin man exited, and when out of Carpozzi's sight, the thin man turned to Sam. "What I would give to spend one night with that broad. I'd be her dog anytime, anyplace."

"Forget it, the boss would kill you." Sammy couldn't stop imagining what it would be like.

"Let's get a beer. I gotta cool down."

Chapter Twenty

It was a cool beautiful autumn day. There was a slight wind, but it was sunny and bright. Q stood in the shadow of the stadium adjusting his sunglasses as he was about to enter his Jaguar convertible. An intern from his football team's public relations department ran up to him. "Mr. Scott, this package came for you, and I was told to get it to you right away."

"Thanks. Looks like some more game film for Monday's game. Wonder why coach didn't give it to me in the locker room? Think I'll wait till I get home to check it out."

On the freeway to his home nestled in the hills with a large lake overlooking his modern ranch-style mansion, Q flicked on the radio and listened to his favorite music station and sang along to *Come In Out of the Rain.*

Life was good for this handsome athlete blessed not only with a great throwing arm, but possessing a winning smile and personality. The team was leading its division, and he was among the six top-rated quarterbacks in the league. He had an adoring wife, three blonde kids and the world loving him. The essence of the perfect couple.

Basically, a family man, he loved his wife, but with his power and the acclaim of his celebrity came almost an obligation to share himself with others, or at least this was the justification for his occasional straying to the arms of his adoring female fans.

Careful to never let his family ever get an inkling of his trysts and certainly never flaunting his actions, he passed himself off as the complete family man.

Q, finding his wife and kids not home, let himself in, petted his dog, grabbed a beer from the fridge, and headed to his den and entertainment center. He placed the tape into his set, pressed the play button, and settled back. The beer bottle burst into a thousand pieces as it hit the large screen as Q hoped to erase the pictures etched into his mind.

"What? How?" Shaking, he grabbed the tape, saw the note attached and paced. This couldn't be happening to him, and why would what was her name—that bitch—do this?

Ten minutes before he was listening to her sing on his car radio.

She had as much to lose as he did. No, the publicity would promote her new CD. His mind was racing in a hundred directions. How could he get in touch with her?

Wait. Maybe she was also getting blackmailed but there was no demand in the note. Of course, that's why the phone number on the tape, but it clearly said not to call for about another 15 hours.

He would be crazy with fear by then. Suddenly he remembered how he met her at the fight in Vegas.

That lawyer knew her. He was the nice guy who represented the fighter who got knocked out. What was his name? Wait…where was that card? Hell he'd never find it. He probably threw it out just as he did a thousand cards before when they were given to him.

Q cleaned up the mess and sat down. He started to call his agent but hung up.

No he would go this alone for the moment. He left a note for his wife that he would be at a team meeting looking at game film and not to wait dinner for him.

The breeze felt good against his face as he wheeled his car onto the freeway and opened the baby up. Maybe just maybe he could outrace what was to come.

Speeding down the freeway, he never noticed the motorcycle resting behind a large billboard until the flashing lights and siren startled him to reality. The officer pulled him over and approached the car carefully.

"Your license and registration card, sir, and stay in the car."

"Yes, sir."

Q searched for his license and registration and also his insurance card.

"Thank you, and please don't open the door," the officer said as he checked the registration card on the computer system mounted on his bike and came toward the Jaguar.

"Mr. Scott, you were speeding and going over the limit by 20 miles an hour. Kindly step out of the car and I will test you for alcohol content as you seemed to be weaving."

He glanced at Q for the first time. "Wait a second, aren't you...? I know you."

"Officer, please I was trying to get some game film for the Monday night game, and if I was going a little fast I apologize. I was trying to figure out some game schemes so we win."

"Well, I guess I could let you go with a warning this time, but you got to slow down. You could hurt yourself or kill someone."

If only the officer knew how close to the truth that was, Q thought and muttered something under his breath.

"What did you say?"

"Nothing, officer. I was thinking out loud. I have a football with me in the rear seat and if you have kids I could autograph this ball."

"Swell yes. Make it to John and Tracy. That would be good, and lots of luck on Monday, and watch how you drive."

"You bet," Q said, handing him the ball.

The officer did follow him for a distance before Q turned off the freeway and headed back home.

Is it any wonder celebrities feel they are entitled to special treatment? The world pays homage to those with special skills like dunking a basketball or throwing a touchdown, not to those who develop medicine, clean streets, or fix toilets. How about the rest of the world, people who work hard, take care of their kids, teach them right from wrong and probably never will be asked to autograph anything in their lifetime except to sign their name to the monthly mortgage payment check. Why me? Q thought. *Lots of people go to Vegas and never get into trouble. It's the price of being a celebrity. How very unfair.*

If Q thought his predicament was unfair, he was about to get a lesson in what unfairness really meant. At the appointed time, he dialed the phone number and a voice answered, "Listen up. This is not a discussion. You are favored to win by

114

six or more points Monday night. You must go under the point spread. No more than five points or you will see that tape all over the Internet and on your favorite talk shows. Your wife will get the deluxe version. You understand?"

"Who are you, and how did you get that tape?"

"No more talking, just listen. Five or less points. There will be no more calls. You control your life. Do this and you'll never hear from me or the tape ever again."

The phone disconnected, and Q stood listening to the dial tone as if that could change the message. The thin man, remembering his instructions, dropped the phone and with his foot stomped it to pieces. Dialing from a different phone, he excitedly exclaimed, "Boss, lunch was delivered and eaten."

Upon receiving the cryptic phone call, Carpozzi went to his bedroom and, on his computer, wrote a list of individuals located across the United States, and next to each name amounts ranging from $50,000 to $200,000 until the total was $5 million.

"The deal is set, and I'm lining up the investors now," he said to each of the callers before telling them the amount of their piece of the action.

"We'll want your investment spread over the next few days, not all at once. I don't want to attract any notice, got it?"

Carpozzi did not want large sums of money to attract attention and affect the betting line of six points. This way the money would be in relatively medium amounts and be coming from across the country at various locations.

"Nobody should be the wiser."

"You sure you got this covered?" came the voice from the other end of the conversation.

"Yes, I'm sure of the outcome. Take it to the bank."

Carpozzi sat back and remembered a movie where a young guy hit on someone else's girlfriend, and when he was discovered and the tough guy who was about to beat him said to the kid, "The juice is worth the squeeze." It took the young guy a while to understand the meaning, and he had to pay the price for the fun he had.

"Even great quarterbacks have to pay for the squeeze," Carpozzi said aloud.

Chapter Twenty-One

Dex was crossing the main street on his way to teach when a steel-gray Mercedes, with honking horn and loud radio blaring, almost ran into him as the driver yelled, "Professor Randle, hey, hold up a minute. I want to speak to you."

Seated in the driver's seat, wearing a Hugo Boss suit with a large diamond stud in his ear, was Trent Prichard.

"Professor, I need to tell you, but I just don't know how to—"

"It's okay. I understand you obviously don't need me to help pick an agent. It looks like you've already got one," Dex said.

"Sir, I have great respect for you, and I really wanted you to represent me after the season, but how can I resist all this and more?" Trent turned around as he lost eye contact with Dex.

"I understand, really I do, and remember if you need me—and you will—I'm here for you. Please be careful. I think you might be in trouble already, and I sure as hell wouldn't be showing off this car and the clothes. Don't even tell me if you signed and with whom. I don't want to know."

Trent looked like he wanted to say more but thought better of it.

The two gave each other one last look, and Trent drove off.

Dex sighed and continued toward the law school, wondering what he could and should have said at their earlier meeting that would have prevented Trent from betraying his team, his school, and worst of all, himself.

"Hurry up, dear. It's getting late, and I really want to get to the cocktail party."

"I need you to zip my dress," Donna said as she moved across the hotel room and stood before her husband, waiting for his approval, not fishing, but what woman doesn't appreciate a compliment from the man she loves?

"You look great. I don't remember that dress. Is it new?"

"I got it last year, but it's still in style. Besides, at these New York charity record parties it doesn't matter what you wear. Everyone outdoes everyone, and anything goes."

Donna was right. The parties were meant to be fund-raisers for some bigwig record executive's favorite charity and an opportunity to network with a who's who of the powers that ran the industry.

Tonight's affair was going to honor Can't Take It with You Records and its CEO Vincent Carpozzi and his favorite charity.

Special guest performer was none other than Val Clifton, and word was that after the performance and the tribute to the wonderful charity work and award that Carpozzi was to receive, he was going to surprise her with a platinum record signifying one million record sales, and in this case a two million records sold, signifying two times platinum.

"Let me fix your tie. It's a little crooked." Donna leaned over and Dex bent forward, kissing his wife.

"I love you."

"Easy does it. Don't mess up my makeup or we'll never get to that boring party."

"One thing is for sure, you can't call them boring. They are lots of other things but definitely not boring," Dex said.

They went into the hall, pressed the elevator button, and descended to the large ballroom already filled with lots of guys dressed like penguins and women with exposed bosoms. Dex loved the action.

Almost immediately, Dex took a butlered glass of champagne with one hand and with the other reached out and shook hands with a record executive he knew from New York.

"How's the city of brotherly love, and why don't you move up here to where the action really is?" said one guy who looked like a penguin with an overstuffed shirt and a plate of food to match.

"Maybe if you give me a big enough advance on that deal you're considering, I could afford to move with the big boys," Dex mumbled as Donna smiled and said hello to the penguin's companion, afraid her husband might say something he was really thinking. Donna marveled at how even tempered her husband was, but took no chances knowing how Dex really felt about self-pretentious blowhards.

Smiling, Dex turned and was off working the crowd when he noticed Trolly in a corner of the foyer. Funny, he never mentioned he was coming tonight. It was natural that he be there but unusual not to tell Dex and not arrange to be seated at the same table.

119

"Hey, Trol. You didn't tell me you were coming."

"Sorry, man. I got a late invite from Val who insisted I make an appearance."

He leaned over and kissed Donna then hugged Dex, and everything was alright between them.

"You believe that jerk getting this award? I don't care if he gives a million to that charity—that SOB."

"Trolly, calm down. Be cool. Let's meet some record guys and get you some production deals while we're here."

Donna stood there as the two took off, but she knew the game and enjoyed watching the excitement and characters as they moved to and fro, shaking hands and vying to be seen.

Dex stopped short in his tracks as he looked up and almost bumped into one of the biggest music agents in the country standing with his arm around Trent Prichard, who was with his fiancée.

"Professor, how are you?"

"Fine."

Before he could say another word, Trent was introducing him to Jeff Barton who leaned forward to give Dex a hug and asked, "How are you? Haven't seen you for a few years."

Dex managed a weak smile in reply.

"Did you know I'm into football as well? Representing this fine guy who should be a first round pick." As he patted Trent on the shoulder, Trent shrugged it off.

"Say, don't you represent some players?" Before Dex could answer, Jeff turned to Trent. "Dex here will tell you, Trent, I'm the best hustler and most active agent you'll ever meet. Ain't that right, Dex?"

"That's true. Nobody is a bigger hustler than your agent," Dex muttered and turned to move away.

Later when he turned back he noticed Jeff was huddled in the corner speaking with Carpozzi and Sammy as if they had known each other for years. Carpozzi was handing Trent a drink, and they were all smiling and taking pictures.

Dex thought Trent still had a couple of games left in his senior year. Arrogance sure begets arrogance and stupidity sure as heck begets stupidity. Jeff, for sure, knew better.

"Arrogance and stupidity, now that's a combination!" mumbled Dex.

The night moved on, and a black-tie waiter carrying a xylophone hit a few notes as he walked through the crowd announcing dinner was being served.

There must have been 600 people being ushered to their tables. Dex and Donna and some others were seated near the back of the room far from the dais.

Dex was used to this as those closest to the honoree paid more for the tickets and probably bought an ad in the program book.

Far up ahead he noticed Sonia, Trent and his new agent at one table and close by were Sammy and some promotion men at another.

Trolly was seated with some people from Can't Take It with You Records, which Dex found interesting, but he was the producer of the hit single *Come In Out of the Rain* and deserved some credit.

Dex made small talk with some of the guests at his table, which also included some free-loading press who, with their credentials, were always present at record events. When they heard he was Trolly's lawyer, they quizzed Dex about rumors of Trolly being an item with Val, and one of the reporters mentioned something about their engagement. Dex assured them it was not true.

As a multicolored dessert, consisting of white chocolate, dark cake and lemon ice was slapped in front of them, the master of ceremonies introduced the head table, made a few remarks, and announced as a special tribute to the honoree that Val was performing her hit single.

"And now ladies and gentlemen, the newest star in the galaxy. Put your hands together and welcome Val Clifton."

The curtain opened behind the dais and Val with three backup singers, six hip-hop dancers and a full fifteen-piece house band entertained the crowd, and when she was about to finish her hit single, from stage's left appeared Dondi-Z with two more rappers who joined Val and blew the audience away singing and rapping to a standing ovation.

The crowd was still screaming and cheering when she then turned to Carpozzi and thanked him for all he had done for her personally and how she supported his charity.

Val then turned and the spotlight followed to the table where Trolly was seated and she thanked her producer and threw him a kiss and asked him to stand and come up on stage with her. Not exactly the politic or smart thing to do on a night they were honoring Carpozzi for his charity work.

Carpozzi came toward her with a large platinum album while the cameras were snapping the scene. Carpozzi stopped momentarily as Trolly took the stage, then regained his composure and hugged Val as he handed her the replica album, which was not really platinum but merely painted that color.

Carpozzi shook hands with Trolly as he watched Val and Trolly embrace with sheer joy.

Later a check for $250,000 was presented by Carpozzi to the executive director of the charity. As Carpozzi got a Lucite statue and received his polite ovation, he couldn't conceal the rage that was building inside.

Donna turned to her husband and quietly shook her head but Dex cut her off before the reporters at the table would hear her say something best left unsaid.

One reporter at the table chuckled and said to Dex. "You sure are on top of your client. The two of them look married, and I don't mean Carpozzi."

The after party where the VIPs mingle and drink, during which everyone tried to attend and be seen was smaller than usual. Dex and Donna searched for their friend and noticeably missing were Val and Trolly. Carpozzi was holding court and greeting well-wishers and appearing gracious but already was searching for Val.

Dex sighed and was relieved when he saw Val emerge from the corridor and immediately walk toward Donna's side as if the two were best friends and had been talking all night.

Grabbing Donna's hand, Val whisked her to where Carpozzi was standing.

"Vincent, please say hello to a dear friend of mine, Donna Randle, Dex Randle's wife. We've been catching up on old times."

Carpozzi coolly eyed Val and turned to Donna. "Yes, I've already had the pleasure but it's nice to see you again."

Carpozzi quickly turned away and was greeted by another well-wisher.

"Damn that could've been bad real bad. Thanks Donna, you saved me a lot of trouble, which I'm already in big time."

Donna looked at the star who just minutes before had wowed the crowd and received a platinum award and could only feel sadness for her.

"Glad to help, but you've got to do something about this triangle before you and Trolly both get killed. Darn I didn't mean to say that." Donna reddened.

Val turned to Donna and hugged her. "Thanks."

Val excused herself and explained she was exhausted and was going back to her room.

Taking this as almost a signal, Donna chimed in, "We were just leaving, so Dex and I will leave with you and see you to your suite."

How is this happening? My wife who didn't want to come in the first place is now a coconspirator to this insanity, Dex thought. He nodded quick good-byes to several nearby guests, and the three headed for the exit.

Chapter Twenty-Two

The elevator ride to Val's floor was filled with conversation between the two ladies laughing and taking turns, discussing the outrageous fashions and levels of cleavage that were exposed. When the threesome came to Val's door, she hugged Donna, kissed Dex on the cheek, inserted her electronic key card in the slot, waited as the green light came on, and quickly entered her suite.

Dex and Donna turned and walked down the hall to await the elevator.

"Don't turn on the light," a familiar voice called out. "Reach for the table and sit down."

Val did as she was told, then a single candle lit the room as Trolly wheeled a room service cart to the table and set out pancakes, syrup, a cut-up pear, and hot tea.

Val squealed with delight. "I'm famished. I haven't had a chance to eat since this morning."

She reached over, squeezed his hand, kissed him lightly on the lips, and said, "Let me change and get out of this dress. These shoes are killing me."

As she entered the bathroom and turned on the light, there already set out on the sink with a pink bow was a pair of sweats and a T-shirt with a logo on the front of a Grammy award and the words *two times platinum* embroidered on the front.

Val quickly scrubbed her face free of makeup, applied some lip gloss, and put her hair in a ponytail. She placed a dash of perfume on her neck and breasts and behind her wrists then slipped into the sweats and T-shirt.

Trolly rose and pulled her chair out as Val sat down and poured a little syrup from a small white pitcher on the pancakes then devoured two or three-bite sized pieces and took a sip of tea.

She took another bite of pancake and looked up in surprise when she bit into something hard. She took it out of her mouth and studied it. "What the heck is this? Oh my God it's a diamond engagement ring?"

"Hope you like it," Trolly said, obviously pleased with the way everything was going. He smiled.

"Like it? I love it. Now I understand the pear on the plate." She held up the sticky three-carat pear-shaped ring toward Trolly who slowly put her finger in his mouth and licked the syrup from her.

She rose, and he noticed her taut breasts under the T-shirt as he drew her close to him and kissed her neck then her lips, tasting the syrup. Her tongue, an intriguing blend of sensual smell and sweetness, darted in and out.

"I love you so much it hurts," Val mumbled.

She raised her arms as the T-shirt was pulled over her head and his tongue explored the crevice between her breasts. He poured the remaining syrup on her nipples and using his tongue, cleaned away the syrup as she moaned.

Her sweats came down and she deftly unbuckled his belt, bent and caressed his manhood.

Trolly stood there motionless with closed eyes and was like a vacuum being sucked into an abyss. He lowered his arms, encircling her and raised her up. He lifted her into him and stroked her back while she rocked back and forth. She then arched, and he pulled her small body into and then away in swift motions, stroking her stomach as she made sounds that excited him even more.

Just when he thought he could not stand it another second, he deftly released her, turned her around, grabbed her, and leaned against her.

Val pushed back against him, and she felt as once as he entered her, bending her over the couch and fondling her while pushing hard against her.

Val gasped for a second and welcomed her lover into her, rapidly moving to accommodate the ever-expanding delight.

The table rattled as if joining in the lovemaking, and both lovers were in that sensual space when the world belonged to them alone as they climaxed together. Trolly pleaded for her not to move because every nerve ending was on fire.

Val laughed and purposely shook again as he pleaded for help. They fell to the couch and embraced the moment when the world only knows peace and serenity.

Every historian knows only too well that when the world knows peace and serenity that it came about as a result of compromise from a prior war and treaty. So as the lovers enjoyed their serenity, other forces were at work that would interfere with and reject their peace. Sun Tzu, several thousand years ago said, "The most brilliant general was the one who won the war without ever having to fight a battle."

Vince Carpozzi was not that brilliant type of general, he had been dishonored and he knew force, pain and revenge were his only fields of battle. His way to show he was, is and shall remain the boss.

In his world, lack of fear equals lack of respect and he could not allow for that weakness. The lovers blissfully enjoying the peace of the night were unaware they were the subject of Carpozzi's hunger for revenge and how he and his crew would mete it out.

Battle plans were being drawn as Val and Trolly fell asleep. It was decided that skirmish would be dealt with after the more promising battle of Monday Night Football, which was fast approaching.

Chapter Twenty-Three

Q had made up his mind that so long as his team won the game, who would care by how many points. Could he control the outcome since he was but one man on the field of twenty-two? The thought pounded in his head as he sat in the locker room waiting for the start of the game.

"Tonight's the night. Play hard on three." The players joined hands in a circle and in unison shouted, "One, two, three, play hard." As each player moved to his own beat, all were unified with the common goal to win. Win at all costs. Isn't that what they are taught from early school yard play, through college and on to the pros? Winning is what makes the paychecks flow.

Monday Night Football is a happening, a celebration attended by thousands of fans, with a national audience of millions more watching on television. Each play is scrutinized by rabid fans who start arriving at the stadium hours in advance to eat, drink and escape their everyday existence. They take the role of their idolized athletes and vicariously live through each and every movement on the field. The world is put on pause during the three hours it takes to play the game, with commercials and breaks totally consuming the public consciousness. Some scream, some pray and some even paint their faces in their team's colors to help the heroes prevail.

This game featured a wide-open offense by Q's team and a tight defense by the other. It was a game in which the talking heads, mostly retired ex-players were in consensus that Q's team would win and should do so by more than six points. The Vegas odds makers had established the spread and believed Q's potent offense would provide that margin of victory.

Q had to figure out how to keep the score low, win the game, and not do so by more than five points to prevent the tape from being broadcasted to his wife and others. Doing as the phone call directed would make the caller disappear with the tape and out of his life, which would then return to normal.

No one had given much thought about the weather and how it could affect the outcome of a game. As the rain cascaded on the field, it made the turf slippery and difficult for the receivers to keep their footing and run their patterns.

Q had thrown for one touchdown and a rushing TD by the fullback accounted for 14 points at the half with the opponents scoring a touchdown and a field goal, giving them a total of ten points.

During halftime, Q sat in the locker room quietly self-absorbed while the coach drew diagrams on the chalkboard filled with X's and O's, exhorting his players to work harder.

"Cover this and be watchful for that, and of course keep thinking on the field," the coach said before he continued to keep the trite sayings going.

"Hold your heads high and be proud," he said as the team exited the locker room. The coach called back Q and said, "You okay? You look a little tight. We need an early score this half to take them out of their game plan."

"Gotcha, Coach, will do."

The third quarter was like a mud bath with each side moving up and down the field. The ball, wet with rain and slippery, was difficult to handle.

In the fourth quarter, a charging defensive player hit Q's arm as he was throwing and the ball took an upward flight and settled in the opposing corner back's hands as he intercepted the errant pass and squished his way back to the thirty-five-yard line. Three plays later, they were on the twenty-seven yard line and on fourth down, lined up and kicked a field goal making the score 14 to 13.

Carpozzi and crew clanked glasses as they settled in for the rest of the game and the big payday. "Wish the gun would go off and our boys collect big," Carpozzi bellowed between sips of scotch.

It was getting close to the two-minute warning, and the coach called time out.

"Q, you got to put points on the board or at least run the ball and eat up time. We can't let them get the ball back with us up only a point."

Q nodded.

Two plays later on third down and with eight yards to go for a first down, Q's coach sent in a play. With well over a minute remaining, if they didn't keep control, the other team would have more than enough time to drive downfield and win with a field goal.

131

A safe short pass designed to make a first down, keep possession of the ball and let the time run out. Q was to run an option play to his right and look for the man coming out of the backfield.

If he was clear, Q would throw him a short pass. If the field was open, Q could scramble for the first down.

Q moved to the line, and as he read the defense, he sensed a rush or blitz coming at him so that if he hesitated even for a few seconds longer, his wide receiver might get open. The coverage would be by a slower safety who the receiver could then outrun and outjump.

Q changed the play at the line, and the ball was snapped to him. Sure enough, the corners charged in as Q gripped the laces of the football with his thumb on the front edge.

Years of training and muscle memory took over, and he pumped his arm as if to throw short as his wide receiver broke for the goal line.

Q planted his back foot, hesitated to give the receiver time to get down field, and threw for an imaginary point ahead of his receiver who was easily in front of the slower and shorter strong safety who had momentarily hesitated when Q pumped his arm and faked the throw.

The ball, in a perfect spiral and rotating, sailed for 20 yards and was picture perfect as it carried just in front of the wide receiver who caught it without breaking stride and sailed into the end zone for a touchdown.

All hell broke loose, and the noise, as thousands of fans screamed in delight, caused the stadium to shake. Fans high-fived and pounded one another. The bench was cleared as the team jumped up and down.

Three teammates jumped on the wide receiver for joy knocking him down in the end zone as Q ran down the field and jumped on the pile of celebrating players.

Carpozzi and his entourage sat frozen for a moment, and it was Carpozzi who threw the phone at the TV. That split-second decision of Q and the touchdown cost him and his friends five million in bets and somebody would pay dearly for the loss. This was his deal, and he would have to make good to those he placed in the action. He could only hope it ended his responsibility and they would leave it at that. This was the way it was in his world, and Carpozzi also had his own score to settle.

"Sammy, get me that little jerk who made the phone call to Q and bring him to me."

"Yes, boss, right away."

When the two men entered the room, Carpozzi stood over his desk and quietly said, "You made the call and told me lunch was served and Q knew what he had to do, right?"

"Yes, sir, he knew, and I did exactly as told."

"Well then he screwed up, so listen closely. One of his kids is having a birthday party next week. Send the kid a gift-wrapped box and put the DVD in the box and sign the birthday card from his daddy."

Carpozzi hesitated then continued, "His wife and kids should love the tape, and if we're lucky, maybe they'll show it in front of a bunch of people at the party. Let the famous quarterback dodge that bullet."

"You got it, boss."

"Don't screw up. I want that bastard to know pain and humiliation. Now get out of my sight." As the door closed,

Carpozzi bellowed, "Sammy, stay here a minute. We got real problems, the least of which is paying back the five mill."

Sammy looked at Carpozzi and understood what he had to do.

"As soon as he takes care of what I told him to do, you take him for a long drive, and I never want to see his ugly face again. Period. Finished."

"Boss, he's my cousin."

One look from Carpozzi, and Sammy turned and walked out.

Chapter Twenty-Four

"Hey, Jer. How you doing? Wife and kids?"

"Doing well, and how's the big-time entertainment lawyer?" Jerry answered into the phone and continued without waiting for a response. "When are we getting together? It's been too long. I thought you might have invited me to lecture at your law school by now."

"I'll do better. Why not give up all that crap you do and come down here full time and teach."

"Never can tell, one day I just might take you up on that offer, but I'll wait till you become dean, and word is I hear it's getting closer. I hear your client hit the big time with her album, and I think I saw an advertisement that she's coming on tour and playing a gig next month near here. Can you scrounge up some tickets for your best friend? Law professors don't make a lot."

"You got 'em. Gotta run. Talk to you soon, and give my love to your wife. Think about my offer, you'd be a lot happier. Later."

Dex always felt better and life was real when he spoke to his old law school buddy and heard his voice.

Nora buzzed Dex on the intercom. "Mr. Randle, Charles Pierce is here for his 11:30 appointment."

"Thanks. Tell him I'll be right there and to have a seat."

Dex got up and walked to the reception area. "Chuck, good to see you and how's the family?"

"Things are good, and you're going to love this project."

Chuck was a producer and sometime director who in his younger day had a small hit TV series and was always trying to regain his glory, pitching and attempting to sell his latest idea.

Dex liked him and would listen to his TV pitches and try to help, but having an idea then translating that to a sold show was a long leap and difficult to do.

Chuck sat down and leaned forward, gathering excitement just talking about the concept for his reality-based comedy show.

"So then Burt, he's the classically trained violinist who plays first violin with the world-famous Philadelphia orchestra, sneaks off after playing the concert and goes to his Texas hold 'em poker game where he plays really high-stakes poker and loses his violin on a bet. Funny, huh?" He didn't wait for Dex to respond. "I got lots of episodes like a scene with a hooker and an episode where he comes in drunk to a rehearsal and plays bebop on his violin and the whole orchestra joins in while the conductor is pulling his hair out."

Chuck paused. "So what do you think? Can you set up a meet with the networks, or is this better for cable?"

Dex paused for a second before answering his friend. "I must've missed something. When did he get back his violin?"

"Don't be wise. Of course he gets it back."

"Did you protect the story and episodes by filing a copyright form and registering it with the Writers Guild of America.?"

"You think it's that good?" Chuck's eyes widened with excitement.

"Regardless, before you shop it around you should protect it first."

"Great. I'll do it, but can you shop it for me?"

Dex reflected for a moment and mentally tried to guess how many times in his twenty-plus years he had heard the same pitch, whether it was a demo record or a movie script or as here a TV project. Too, too many to even count. Everyone believed they would write that great bestseller or produce a Grammy album or sitcom hit.

Chuck was his friend, and over the years, he developed a warm feeling for the older man, so he tried to be delicate. "Put together a more fleshed-out description of some of the weekly episodes, make them real and funny and get back to me, and we'll decide the next step."

"Thanks, and I'll call in a week or so. See ya."

Dex knew he meant it and would be back or call the following week.

Imagine if I ever charged these guys, I could have retired at forty-five. Boy, if life were only that easy, Dex thought and settled into the mound of mail piled in front of him.

In the pile of mail, faxes, and memos was a copy of an Internet article with a headline, QB TAKES PERSONAL LEAVE FROM TEAM.

The article went on to describe that Darrell Scott, the quarterback affectionately known as Q wasn't so affectionately admired by his wife who had filed for divorce. Q had done an unprecedented act by requesting a personal

137

leave from his team while they were in first place in their division. There was no mention of when he would return.

Wow, Dex thought, *must be more than meets the eye to that story.*

In the same pile was a BMI statement for Trolly, which was a computer printout of the last quarter of various performance payouts resulting from on-air plays such as radio and television, and other sources of income from the songs on which Trolly as the writer and publisher of his music would receive royalties.

The statement reflected that most of the payments came from radio airplay of Val's *Come In Out of the Rain*, and the enclosed check was in the low six figures.

Dex picked up the phone and dialed Trolly. "Yo, go get that two-seater you been eyeballing. You just got a nice royalty statement and check, which I'm sending over to your accountant for deposit," Dex said.

"Thanks. Val's been out on tour again, and I really miss her." Trolly never even asked the amount of the check. "Funny how the love of my life is really paying for that sports car, isn't it?"

"Hey easy, man, you helped write the song and you produced it, so enjoy the car, unless of course I can convince you to invest the money for your future. If you invested that check and got six percent in twelve years, it would double and in twelve more years, that sum would double again. Not too shabby."

"Dex, some days I don't think I have a future, it could be my last twelve days, let alone twelve years. Word on the street is Carpozzi is really pissed about that awards dinner and Val

138

sharing the stage with me and even more about the engagement."

"He's not that stupid to do something."

"I'm really scared for Val. You hear about that quarterback you met in Vegas?"

"Yeah, just read about it, why?"

"Val told me something in strict confidence, and it would blow your mind. Let's drop the subject."

"You brought it up."

"Please forget I said anything, I got some real bad feelings. Let me get back to you, and thanks for your call. You're right, I really wanted that two-seater."

Chapter Twenty-Five

Dinner that night was relaxing. The boys were questioned about school. "Learn anything new?" Dex got the usual short responses.

"Nothing much," Brett said.

Brett was talking about sports and Jamie was suspiciously quiet. Donna was wrapped up in some charity event she was planning. Plates were cleared, and the boys went to their rooms or wherever and Dex, after coffee with Donna, moved to his den, grabbed a magazine, and turned on the TV.

"Hey, Dad, whatcha doing?" Jamie asked a few minutes later.

"Not much. What's up?"

"Dad, I need to ask you something, okay?" Jamie said as he closed the den door.

"Sure, son. Sit down. What's on your mind?"

"Dad, I need some advice, but you've got to promise me it won't affect our driving lesson and my applying for my learner's permit."

"You got it."

Jamie had just turned 16 and like every teenager, that was the magical moment when every thought turned to driving. Dex was ready for the talk to center on the purchase of a used car or whatever but Jamie had other problems to discuss.

He looked at his dad and hesitated. Even though he loved his father and all his buddies thought Dex was the coolest of fathers, this was different.

"Now don't get pissed at me. I didn't do anything but you know my girlfriend Lisa well…"

Dex interrupted, "Son, you're much too young…" He stopped short and thought, *Damn, why did I interrupt?* "Sorry, please finish."

"Dad, see you're already jumping to conclusions."

"You're right. Sorry please…"

"Lisa is really great, and I really like her, really a lot but lately when we go to parties, especially because I play on varsity and I'm only a freshman, the older guys are hitting on Lisa, and well she and everyone else are drinking beer and doing sugar cubes and nose candy and pills and—"

"Woah," Dex interrupted, "sugar cubes? Where do you come to that?"

"Dad, let me finish. I don't do that stuff, but all the guys are passing stuff around, and Lisa thinks I'm chicken, and—"

Dex thought back to his younger days and his philosophy which he still tried to follow of his apple pie theory of life. Each person is in essence an apple pie or any pie and you took slices and divided life into pieces—a piece for sleeping, eating, loving, working, and the trick of a good life was to balance the pieces so you covered all areas.

You didn't cross over the balances and rob one sector by taking too big a slice and hurting the other slice. This pie of life was not the right speech for this problem, no matter how small a slice, he didn't want his sixteen-year-old experimenting with booze and drugs. He needed more to say.

141

"Dad, Dad, Dad, you listening to me?"

Dex was jarred back to reality. "My son…"

Before he could say another word, Jamie knew he was about to get a lecture.

Dex paused. Not so much for effect, this wasn't the courtroom but he wasn't sure how to make his words meaningful to his son. Every parent has known this experience. "Jamie, as you grow older, more and more decisions become difficult, and that's the way it should be. It's what growing up and becoming your own person means. It also means you have to decide how you want your life to go as a follower, which is often the easy way or as a leader or individual who does what he thinks best for himself and what he knows is right, which is often the hardest choice to make.

"I can tell you this, every choice causes a result, sometimes not a very big one. Other times a seemingly small choice can have dire results because they cause other actions to follow, which are not contemplated."

Dex paused to see if he was losing his son, but Jamie was listening so he continued. "Taking a drug alone might not matter, but if it causes you to do something or react in a way you shouldn't, it can change your whole life direction. A simple beer isn't the end of the world, but if it causes you to cause a car accident, it can affect your whole life. You might wonder what one pill is gonna do, but if it causes you to do something under its influence you wouldn't normally do, what then?

"Lisa is a lovely young lady but her actions here can result in stupid behavior leading to real trouble. If not following the crowd causes you to lose her now rather than in a few months or later, so be it. It's probably for the better, but—and this is important—it's your call, son, your decision. I only know every action, however small starts a chain reaction in life."

Dex paused then continued, "Mom and I have tried to instill good basics and hopefully some guidance based on our own learning from mistakes and experiences. Guidance helps but the choice is yours."

Jamie stared at his dad and without a word reached over and hugged him. He stood and opened the door and started to exit before turning back. "Thanks, Pop, and could we keep this to ourselves? Mom doesn't have to be in on this conversation, okay?"

"You got it, Son."

Later that night as Dex and Donna were preparing for bed, Donna asked, "So what were you and Jamie talking about, and why did he close the door?"

"Nothing much, just some man-to-man advice."

Donna stared at her husband, guessing the conversation was about Lisa. "Did he get to kissing and petting yet?"

"Hey, he's only sixteen." Dex rolled over, which signaled the end to the conversation.

Chapter Twenty-Six

"Of course I understand. No one likes to lose money. Yes, it will all be made good." Carpozzi's low and measured tone highlighted the importance of whoever he was speaking to on the other end of the phone. "Can't believe he threw that touchdown himself." Carpozzi continued, "She is still on tour, and her record sales are goin' great. She's even starting to make a profit on the road."

The voice on the other end spoke and Carpozzi listened.

"Yes, I hear and understand. No, she'll never see any of that money, but that bitch is gonna earn it all back plus."

The call ended and Carpozzi slumped into his chair, clicked on the computer, reviewed the list of illegal payoffs he had advanced to get airplay, and then looked at the list of bets wagered, which he knew he was going to be forced to make good if he had any chance to stay alive. In the pecking order of life, he was up there but even he understood to those above he was expendable.

Pouring a shot of single malt scotch, he gulped it down and felt it burn into his stomach as he cursed his stupidity at getting others involved in the bets and guaranteeing the payoff. He had been so sure of his scheme and how it would curry favor with certain friends that there was no turning back in returning their losses.

The record company profits on Val's album could cover the payback but how to conceal it would need some ingenuity. He took another gulp of scotch and talked to himself.

"There is no way that unfaithful bitch after all I've done for her is ever going to realize a dime. She owes me big time." He figured it was just a matter of time before the producer got his reward. Perhaps he would do it himself. Carpozzi would enjoy seeing Trolly suffer.

Carpozzi picked up the phone and called Sammy on his cell phone. "How's the tour going?"

"Great, boss. She is really packing them in."

"How are concessions doing?"

"Boss, every fan wants a T-shirt or a picture of her wet T-shirt 'Coming In Out of the Rain'. That was a genius idea."

"When this leg of the tour ends, I've got something you'll love doing, and sorry about your cousin."

"Thanks. I understand it had to be done."

Life on the road for a touring artist is not easy. Preparation of a tour is like a logistical military operation with advance planning needed to coordinate the show and all that it entails. Added to that, is the physical condition that a recording artist needs to play a two or three hour show, singing and dancing. Often a star can lose five to ten pounds at a time during a show.

While on tour, sleeping time was at a minimum so it was no accident that Val, at the conclusion of that night's show, was slumped in the limo taking her back to her suite. She entered her room just as the phone was ringing and got it on the third ring.

"Hi, darling. I miss you too. I'm exhausted. The shows are going well, but no don't come out on the road. I don't want Vince more upset than he already is. I think it's five more dates. I don't even remember. You know when you hear an artist open an act by saying 'Yo, Detroit,' and everyone cheers the hometown? Well I now understand how you can be in Milwaukee and think it's Detroit. You get so exhausted, the towns get mixed up.

"Try doing a gig till ten-thirty, getting on a tour bus for six hours, driving to a new town, resting for a few hours, doing a sound check, going back to the hotel, then performing and doing it all over again and again. You forget where you are."

Trolly listened and said, "The life of a star, that's what you dreamed about dear. I've been there, seen it, done it and know how tough this is for you."

"Yes, I love the roar of the crowd and all the adulation but when this tour ends, let's escape and go away. Just you and me forever. I love you. Good night."

"Me too, always."

Val hung up the phone, reached for some sleeping pills, called the operator to place a do not disturb on her phone, undressed, and ran the hot water for a bath.

Sammy was downstairs in the coffee shop with the promoter of that night's performance, haggling about the number of paid attendees and trying to figure how much of a percentage of the gate they were entitled to over and above the flat fee for the evening.

"Val's contract was to be paid a flat fee of $25,000 a night plus a split of the gate based on the numbers. She was also entitled to forty percent of all merchandise sold at the performance from sale of T-shirts, programs, and posters after first deducting cost of goods sold."

"I know what the contract says," the promoter replied.

"Hey, man, don't tell me there were 3,500. It was more like 5,000 in the seats, and we didn't authorize all those comp tickets to the press. Everybody and their mother was showing press credentials and requesting free comp tickets. No way. Pay the percentage on 4,500, and next time she comes back you'll be the promoter for that gig next year."

A young man, dressed in T-shirt, shorts, and work boots approached Sammy. "The gear's all packed and on its way to the next gig, and we're pulling out tonight to get there for tomorrow's show."

"Why don't you sleep over and hit the road early tomorrow instead? You look tired."

"It's okay. We'll take turns sleeping in the truck. See you tomorrow."

"Man, I don't know how these kids do it. I guess you gotta be young and love this stuff," Sammy said to the promoter.

"Yeah, but look at all the tail they get on the road. It's worth it." Both men laughed.

The following morning a knock on the door by room service awakened Val who nibbled on toast, jam, and hot tea with honey while she dressed. She had placed her luggage outside of her door the night before so the road manager could do an early pickup and get everyone's bags loaded onto the truck. She put her night clothes in her carry-on bag and awaited Sammy to come and pick her up to head off to the next city. Five to go and she was home free.

Val had carefully made certain the engagement ring Trolly had given her the night of the charity award dinner was only worn when she was at home. Both had agreed it would only serve to inflame the situation with Carpozzi if he knew and they would wait until after the tour to make any announcements.

Val had taken the ring with her on tour and when back in the privacy of her suite, she would put it on, and as she spoke to Trolly on their nightly phone call would roll it on her finger.

The night before when she came in so exhausted she placed the ring on her finger, hung up from her phone call, took a hot bath and fell almost immediately into a drugged deep sleep.

In the rush to pack and get ready for the next leg of the trip she absentmindedly rushed to the waiting limo and when she arrived to the swarms of paparazzi and photographers she waved to them unaware that the photos of her waiving hand would set off a chain of events that would change the lives of many.

The following day all the major newspapers and one gossip magazine carried stories of Val's left hand and her engagement ring.

One newspaper had a 900 number readers could call for 50 cents and vote for who the lucky guy was from a choice of four candidates. The list of candidates included Will 'Trolly' Turner, Vincent Carpozzi and the recently separated quarterback Darrell 'Q' Scott.

Carpozzi was having lunch and reading the *Daily News* newspaper when he saw the picture of Val and tore it from the paper. Clutching the crumpled picture, he threw it on the floor and picked up his cell phone.

Chapter Twenty-Seven

Val's tour was going well with screaming fans applauding her every song. The band had become very tight, and they played as a seasoned unit, responding and feeding off one another's energy. Bands on the road become a close knit family and spending so much time together causes the real world to submerge into the fantasy of the close knit group excluding all others. Each day then night began another cycle in which the star and group were all that mattered, and the everyday world events lost importance. Newspapers and TV were only used for the write-ups and reviews of how they did in their last gig.

With two weeks left on the road, Val was treated as the queen bee and head of her own state, even her own nation, and it gave her little time to think of the reaction Carpozzi might have and how he would act.

Val, even as her little group closed to protect her, began to think all would be well. She felt that perhaps, with her success, Carpozzi would forgive her and accept her as a double platinum recording artist and understand she was entitled to fall in love. Val rehearsed her lines for the eventual confrontation with Carpozzi.

"You'll always be special to me, and how can I ever thank you for all you've done for me and my career?" She would then kiss his cheek and add, "I hope you're happy for me that I've found true love."

She'd show him the engagement ring, explaining she didn't tell him because she didn't want the announcement interfering with his big night and his award and charity dinner.

Maybe he would even want to throw a big engagement party where they would invite scores of record people and press, which would boost record sales even higher. The road can do that to you and let you fantasize about how wonderful life is and can be. Many artists will tell you after coming off the road of the let down and depression they experience getting back to normal living and Val would be no exception.

Trolly, who missed Val, had been busy back in his recording studio rehearsing and producing a four-person male R-and-B group who had recently signed with a major label. Producing had taken his mind off his personal situation with Carpozzi, and he gave very little thought to his own safety. When Dex and he discussed the situation, he curtly cut the matter and refused to listen, instead changing the subject to his missing Val and producing this new group.

"Listen I'm just saying you need to be careful, that's all."

"Cut it out. Nobody is gonna do anything, and besides I'd like to take a swing at Carpozzi myself. You think he'd louse up all the money his record company is making? No way," Trolly said but the thought had occasionally crossed his mind that he did have a powerful enemy.

"Well just don't go and inflame the situation any more than you already have."

"Yes, boss man," Trolly joked in a high-pitched voice signifying this conversation was closed.

Dex got off the phone and thought maybe, just maybe, he was thinking as a friend and lawyer and not as a businessman.

Even Carpozzi wouldn't disrupt his money-making machine. Dex would have let the conversation go, but all at once, he got that sick feeling in the pit of his stomach and queasy intuition he hated that told him all was not well.

Sara leaned in his office. "Prof, I'm going downstairs for a quick lunch. You want me to get you something?"

"No, thanks. I'm not very hungry. I'll just get some tea to settle my stomach."

"Sure. How about a soft pretzel?"

"No thanks, but here's ten, my treat. I'm getting ready for class. What are we up to this week?"

"You're lecturing on taking a group of artists on the road for a tour and all it entails. The class also has to negotiate a promotion contract."

Dex smiled and thought, *Not all that it entails. Nobody would believe it anyway.*

Chapter Twenty-Eight

Val was enjoying the tour, and as the last gig of the current leg of the tour approached, she was experiencing the duality of sadness as it was drawing to a close and the anticipation and happiness of returning to Philly and being with Trolly.

Fans traditionally flock to the last performance of a tour knowing it would be a while till they could see the artist perform again, while also realizing the last show was something special.

The star put it all out there for her fans and the good-byes always included a special something for the fans to remember. The last night of Val's tour was no exception.

The final gig was filled with all the hits, and when finally some hour and twenty minutes later, Val came back for a standing ovation as she broke into *Come In Out of the Rain*. The crowd was in a near frenzy.

As Val was singing, Dondi-Z appeared and danced over to Val and joined in singing and rapping the chorus, while the crowd had to be restrained from coming on stage.

It was a night Val would always savor, and as each band member signed off with a solo riff, the applause kept growing.

Tired but exhilarated, Val climbed into the limo but quickly changed her mind, exited, and chose instead to ride back to the hotel in the bus with the band members, road crew, and even the groupies acquired for the night. As the bass player groped two groupies he momentarily paused and said aloud.

"Hey, boss lady, when we going back out?"

"Soon as we can," came the reply.

"You really knocked 'em dead."

"Yeah, did you hear them screaming?"

"What a show."

Val sat back and took it all in and loved the comments, loved the world and just loved life that night.

The plane ride back to Philadelphia was uneventful, and as Val disembarked and walked up the ramp, she was greeted by Trolly holding a dozen white roses. They exchanged a long embrace as scores of photographers snapped pictures and asked for quotes and sound bites.

Val waived to the crowd and was hastily maneuvered to a waiting limo. Val kicked off her shoes, snuggled next to Trolly, and relaxed for the first time in weeks, content to close her eyes and not speak.

Once inside Trolly's house, they embraced and hand in hand went to the kitchen.

"Whatcha got to eat? I'm famished," she said.

"How about a grilled cheese and bacon with tea and honey?"

"Love it."

"Coming up, a Trolly special. You go and change, and I'll bring it up to you."

Two people being normal in an abnormal world, Val thought as she ran the water for a hot bath. Several minutes later Trolly appeared with food in hand.

"It's great to be back, I really missed you."

Trolly placed the tray in front of his bedroom fireplace, and as Val pulled the napkin, an envelope fell to her lap. She opened it to find two airline tickets to Costa Rica, with a destination to a very private little resort overlooking the beach.

"We leave in two days for a week, and no excuses. Your tour is over, no studio sessions are booked, and off we go, alone at last." Trolly said as he lifted her up and kissed her as she took a bite of the grilled cheese.

"It's great." She smiled at him. "The sandwich, of course. What about my clothes?"

"Take as few as possible. You won't have much need for your clothes if I have my way," he said, smiling in return.

The next morning when Val entered her apartment, she barely had time to listen to her messages as she packed her bags. She scheduled a hairdresser appointment and massage for that afternoon and was going to be picked up by Trolly who had booked a suite at the airport hotel under an assumed name.

Early the following morning they would be in the air, flying to a private villa and away from the world.

Repeated calls from Sammy to Val went unanswered, and when nobody seemed to know where she was, Sammy rather than see Carpozzi face-to-face preferred to call him giving reports of his efforts to locate her.

"Bring her to me when she shows up," Carpozzi insisted.

"Boss, it's like she disappeared from the face of the earth. Even her band members don't know nothing."

The villa with its thatched ceiling provided escape from the heat of the sun but was porous enough to allow the light to filter in, and it was a paradise to behold. A private, small pool adjoined the sliding glass door of the villa and a patio filled with flowers of all colors added to the beauty and serenity of the lush hideaway.

Val and Trolly dipped their legs in the pool as they sipped champagne and fed each other strawberries.

"Wonder if it ever rains down here?"

Val almost was purring as she slipped out of her bathing top and stretched across the surface of the mats adjacent to the pool.

Almost on signal, Trolly gently poured some champagne on her, then leaned across her body and savored the taste of her.

Val moaned and ascended to meet his body, and together they melded as she spread her legs and he entered her. They experienced not lust, not passion, but love.

Afterward they put their bathing suits on and walked on the private beach, watching the calm blue waters slowly come in and tickle their toes then retreat, each wave going back to the larger ocean and merging to one continuous line as it met the horizon.

Just as the waves came in and then went back, Val and Trolly also had to retreat and roll back to reality, as the week had come to an end.

The two had decided that when they returned to Philly, they would no longer stay apart, but would face the crowds and the press together.

Trolly had convinced Val that Carpozzi needed to be dealt with, and together they would meet with him and tell him their plans. What those plans were and how they would deal with the situation had not really been figured out. They did know whatever the situation, it was going to be dealt with together.

Trolly decided to call Dex and find out what he was doing and if he had any suggestions or advice for the returning couple.

"Hey, man, how's it going?"

"Where the hell are you, and are you with Val?"

"Yes of course, and we're flying home tomorrow."

"Sammy has been searching high and low for Val, and word on the street is Carpozzi is looking for you."

"Well tomorrow he's gonna find me alright, and I'm not gonna pussyfoot with him."

"Hey, you better take it easy."

"You know how I feel about you, and you're my closest friend but nothing you say will change my mind. You got any suggestions?"

"Let's talk when you get back, and maybe we can figure something out to make this come out right."

"Dex, it is right, and I plan to let Carpozzi understand he can't do anything to stop us."

"Talk to you tomorrow."

Trolly decided not to mention the phone call to Val so he wouldn't upset her.

Somehow when they arrived in Philly, there was no one to greet them. Val, with dark glasses and hair tucked under a baseball cap and little makeup, went unnoticed. Unnoticed that is, till a skycap handling the baggage while taking it to a cab saw Trolly and recognized him and the lady he was walking arm in arm with. "Hey Sammy, it's John, you know at the airport. You still looking for that chick? Well she just landed and I'm taking her bags to a cab. You want I should find out where she's headed? I'll call as soon as I hear where when she tells the cabbie and you won't forget me right?"

"Yes, and call me right away and I got you covered man."

Trolly handed the skycap a ten as he held the door for Val, who looked momentarily at Trolly and when asked where she should be taken, gave her address. Val was alone when she entered the cab and Trolly kissed her good-bye before the cab departed. The next cab moved forward and Trolly handed the skycap another ten and entered the cab as his bags were placed in the trunk. "Thanks man."

As the cab took off, Sammy's phone rang, "She got in the cab alone and the other dude got in a separate cab and also left."

"Where did she say she was headed?"

"Couldn't tell, but she left alone."

"Thanks, and I won't forget this." Sammy placed a call. "She's back. Don't know for sure, okay. Boss, no problem."

Chapter Twenty-Nine

"Yes, I understand and I'm sorry," Val said into the phone, which had been ringing almost as soon as she entered her apartment. Sammy blasted, "The man is pissed and I'm trying to save your butt!"

"Of course I realize he's upset and I should have called but I just wanted to get away."

"Lady, get ready, I'm on my way."

"I'm exhausted can't we wait till tomorrow? Okay, I'll be ready, half hour, or should I take a cab over to his house? No, calm down."

"Listen to me, be ready, I'm picking you up, and I don't care what you look like. He wants to see you now."

Val got off the phone and her instinct was to phone Trolly, but she thought better of it. Perhaps she could explain her disappearance to Carpozzi and calm the whole thing down.

She hastily applied lipstick, got redressed and went to the lobby to await Sammy and the limo. Sammy picked up Val in his car and they spoke very little, listening mostly to the car radio as Sammy switched from one station to the next till he found some easy listening station playing Frank.

When they arrived and were admitted to the entrance, Val walked to the study and awaited Carpozzi who was still upstairs taking a shower.

She walked around his desk to pour herself a drink and noticed his computer was on and open to a long list of payments made out to many names and station executives and the heading at the top of the list in italics was *VAL CLIFTON*.

Scrolling down to the next page, she found another list of payments made or sums wagered on the Darrell Scott game, which she didn't understand. Another page had records sold and receipts paid on what she thought was her CD sales, but she was too anxious Carpozzi would appear any second to study the sheets. Instead, she took a blank disk and downloaded the information, then quickly wrapped it in a scarf and placed it in her pocketbook. At that precise moment in time, Val took a step that was one of the turning points which would change her life and that of many others.

Quickly pouring a drink, she looked up as Carpozzi entered the room.

"Good evening, my dear, so nice to see you. Don't you have a lovely tan?"

"Vince, I—"

"No need to explain," he said, cutting her off. "Love does many things to people. So what are your plans for the future?"

Oh God, Val thought, *this is going to be terrible, so brace yourself girl.*

"Might I join you for a drink?" Carpozzi moved toward the desk to pour himself a drink and stopped in front of the computer, looked quizzically at the screen for a long second and closed it.

"Please sit down," he said, settling into a large leather chair opposite the couch where she sat. "So tell me about the vacation and your week? Did you go alone?" He didn't wait for a response. "Of course not. It was that producer guy. I guess it was business?"

"Vince, please let me explain—"

"I don't think you need to. I took you from nowhere—nothing—the streets and gave you everything, made you a star. This is how you repay me?"

"Please let me—"

"Listen to me, slut. From now on, you do as you're told, and don't even call or talk to this Trolly guy or you can kiss off everything."

Val thought perhaps she could calm him down as she slowly stood and walked toward him. She bent down in front of him and recognized the desire welling up in him.

Men are so easy, she thought as she started to put her hand on his chest when suddenly he reached out and slapped her hard across the mouth, and she tasted a trickle of blood.

"Get out of my sight. You think I'd touch you after you've been with him?" Carpozzi turned and walked out, while Val sobbed.

Two men appeared and roughly escorted her to the front door. One of the men handed her a ten-dollar bill, slapped her on the ass, and said, "Take a cab or bus girlie, but get the hell out of here and don't ever come back."

Hours later, tired and cold, Val reached home having been on bus and taxi, before finally reaching a friend by phone to pick her up at a late-night diner.

Val understood that night's meeting with Carpozzi was just the beginning, but she wasn't sure just what he had in mind. She was sure he would not ruin a profitable business venture and she would still be put on tour and then in the recording studio again to follow up on her successful CD.

She figured Carpozzi wouldn't deliberately cut a stream of income, and if nothing else, she was sure she was at the very least that to Can't Take It with You Records.

Val decided it was best not to tell Trolly any of the events that had just transpired and indeed took a hot bath, prepared hot tea and honey, turned on the TV, and exhausted, she moved to her bed.

Moments later, she awoke with a start, jumped from the bed and ran to her pocketbook where she unwrapped the scarf and held the computer disc close to her heart, before placing it inside a book and then carefully placing the book back on the shelf.

As she leaned back on the bed, Val reflected on what had just transpired at Carpozzi's and realized she had more to worry about than she had first imagined. He had turned her down and hit her, which had never before happened.

Next one of his men had patted her on the rump, and though she understood many would want to bed her and probably expressed in vile terms her body parts, none would have dared touch her out of fear of their boss and his retribution unless they had his permission. She was thrown out of the house she, a million dollar property, handed a ten-dollar bill and told to hit the road, knowing there was no easy way for her to get home.

Val had the sense that real serious trouble was coming. She again got up, went to the book, and got the disc.

"Okay, what do I do with this? Who can I trust?"

Val went through everyone she could think of, quickly eliminating Trolly who with his quick temper could not be relied upon. Family was out, and then she knew.

Val moved to the left corner of her bed, picked up the teddy bear, hugged it, pulled open the zipper, and carefully wrapped the disc in a soft towel and placed it in the zipper pocket.

Rummaging through her night stand drawer, she found Dex's business card. Quickly dressing, she took the teddy bear and several of her CDs and went out into the chilly night air.

Chapter Thirty

Almost immediately after her departure from Carpozzi's, he had returned to the office, turned on his computer, and, with adding machine at hand, was determining the sales figures of Val's CD.

The actual U.S. sales exceeded two million, and foreign sales added close to another million or so. Throwing in the record company's share of publishing income, merchandising, and ancillary streams of income, it probably amounted close to $18 million or so, minus about two and a half million owed on royalties to Val and Trolly.

He could easily repay the five million he was responsible for and was sure that once he squared the debt plus some vig of another million to keep his friends happy, he would be fine and left alone.

He had already determined the lovers had forfeited by their actions any rights to their royalty stream of income, and legal or not, they would never see a cent. Nobody messed with Carpozzi and got to profit, he would see to that. He could easily establish a second set of books that would show lower sales figures, a practice not uncommon in the record industry. Also if he manipulated the returns of records that stores returned to the company as charge backs, he could further reduce the profit picture.

Taking away their royalty income was not enough. They needed more punishment than money loss for the insult to him, and to maintain his power and respect, he must do what was demanded of him to keep fear intact, to retain absolute control.

Sun Tzu would be proud of Carpozzi's thinking, he would let the world know, but not prove he was responsible for all that was to occur. No one must be able to tie Carpozzi to whatever was planned.

Once again timing and geography, being at the right place and at the right time, must be planned and executed with precision.

The best revenge should take time, when it hurts the most. When your enemy thinks he or she has escaped and relaxes.

Carpozzi carefully plotted his course of action and when the time was right, the world would know not to mess with him.

He sat back and couldn't help but think of Val and that maybe he should have screwed her one last time, but that would have been a sign of weakness. No, he was ready to move on.

"Sammy," he yelled into the hall, "come in here. What was the name of that good-looking singer?"

"Which one, boss?"

"The one you liked with the big boobs. She was in about a week ago."

"Oh, Carol something or other, but you didn't like her voice."

"Hell, with the voice, I want to see her now. Tell her Mr. Carpozzi will send a limo for her and to bring a change of clothes."

Sammy moved to get her number as Carpozzi went upstairs to prepare for another audition—this time in his bedroom.

Sara sat at her desk in Dex's office and sorted the incoming mail, which she placed in the inbox since Dex liked to open the mail himself.

All demo packages, which were easily identified by their FedEx, UPS, or standard yellow mailing envelopes were opened by her or the interns.

The procedure was to log in each and every demo package on a computer list by name or cross-referenced by any other contact person. If it was an already established client it was quickly reviewed, then placed by number in stored large containers for retrieval if Dex asked for it.

The new or unsolicited demo packages were put into piles, and Sara or the other interns would listen to the music and grade them on a scale from one to ten on a prepared checklist for originality, production quality, and artistic merit.

Occasionally when something was really good Sara would put it into the inbox for Dex to listen to, and if the group really liked it or thought it had potential, Dex might then call back the contact person. The chances were about one in seventy-five or higher that such a call would be made. Most entertainment lawyers could spend their entire billable day listening to demos and never get any work done if they listened to every demo submitted.

Dex had stressed to his group that each submission, however bad it might be, was still the hopes and dreams of the artist submitting it and deserved their attention.

Sara opened a large package from Val Clifton, opened one end, saw several CDs roll out, placed the recordings back in the package, numbered and placed it in one of the Val Clifton files. This was nothing unusual as many artists would send in a number of their CDs for storage, in case Dex wanted to present it to a publicist or attempt to get an endorsement deal or send it to a prospective agent or record company.

What was unusual was that Sara failed to mention to Dex that Val had sent in the package, but she had really breaking news that she knew Dex would want to know right away and that was the only thing on her mind as he appeared in front of her desk.

"Good morning, Sara, how's it going?" Dex asked when he came in. "Anything good in the mail?" He bent over to retrieve his mail.

"Prof, sit down. I have some really bad news."

Dex hated it when people prefaced something they had to say with a statement of whether it was good or bad. "Just tell me, and don't be so darn dramatic."

"Trent Prichard got caught taking money and a car from his agent before he had played his last two or three games, and the university is being penalized for those games, forfeiting their standing. They may be expelling Trent and suing the agent." She paused to catch her breath. "Not only that but—"

Dex cut her off. "How do you know all this? It's not on the news."

"My roommate interns in the general counsel's office at the university, and she overheard them all talking."

"Wow, that is bad. Do you know when the story breaks? Does Trent know any of this?" Dex found himself spitting out question after question, and Sara shook her head and waved her hands, signifying she didn't know.

Dex told Sara to let him know if she heard anything more, then he looked at her and said, "Thanks."

She nodded, got up, and left his office as he leaned back in his lawyer's chair to think.

Chapter Thirty-One

Val returned to her apartment and pressed the message button on the answering machine, and it played three similar calls, all from Trolly. "Baby, I love you. Please call on your return."

The last two messages seemed more urgent, but Val did not return his call. She picked up and put back the phone three or four times, hesitating, not knowing what to say.

Yes, she loved him but she feared Carpozzi and what he might do.

Val was also concerned that if she disobeyed, her career was over. Could she ever go back from where she came and to the filth and poverty of her previous life?

The answer was easy when she thought of the week she spent with Trolly and how happy the two of them were but the confusion of the situation returned.

She was tired and depressed. Reaching for a bottle of wine, she opened it and poured a glass halfway and took a long sip, trying to figure out what to do.

Val moved to the living room and opened a drawer to her wooden chest and pulled a large scrapbook filled with her clippings. There was picture after picture of her posing with celebrities. No, she would never give this up. It was unfair of Trolly at the height of her career for him to want to settle down and keep her from further stardom, but was love and security the price she had to pay for celebrity?

"Why can't I have both?" she wondered aloud.

The next morning, she decided to call Carpozzi and beg for his forgiveness. She could convince him to satisfy his needs and want her. He would put her back in the studio and she would have an even bigger hit, and success would grow.

That night was the first time he had ever turned her advances down. Carpozzi had slapped her, and with his terrible temper, he just might not take her back, then what would she do?

Val got up and moved to her bathroom cabinet to a small vial that contained her sleeping pills. She removed the top, took two small pills, and washed them down with the wine. She would work it all out in the morning.

Trolly, sitting in his studio, was trying not to think of Val. He intently played with the buttons on his twenty-four track recording board and was soon engrossed in laying down tracks of a new song that kept playing in his head. He, like many of the great musicians and producers could not read or write music, but could clearly hear and play a tune in his head.

He heard the melody line and was scribbling the lyrics as he put computer music parts to the track. Each different musical instrument added to the overall effect of the song. It was like giving birth to a new baby, creating a sound and then a song from his inner being, and this was what he loved doing, possibly even more than his love for Val.

As he finished the track, he redialed Val's number and let it ring several times and still got no answer. He got up from the board and walked over to his mini kitchen and made a peanut butter and jelly sandwich, poured hot coffee, and sat down absentminded to read the sports section of the *Daily News*. He was not going to sit there all night and wait. He decided to give it another hour and he was going to Val's apartment. He called again and still there was no answer. This was not the way it was supposed to be. He finally found happiness with one whom he could share his secrets with and would be there for him. He understood he could make her happy, and their shared love of music gave them a common purpose. He was sure that feeling could sustain and surmount many minor differences. But the big question was, were these minor or irreconcilable? He couldn't wait until she heard the new song he had composed just for her.

Trolly listened to the recorded tracks on the loudspeakers then switched the track to a small speaker mounted on the board, and as the lower volume came through, he smiled.

This song was a hit. A trick he learned long ago was to play the song not through the loudspeakers of the studio where everything sounds good, but to use an ordinary car radio speaker. If the song sounded good coming through the small speakers, then he knew it was a hit.

He closed his eyes and remembered his old high school days when he and his two buddies would sing and mimic the groups of the day. They would get together, harmonize, and dream.

"One day I'll be even more famous than they are, and you watch I'm gonna have lots of gold records and have a big car and people will recognize me and say there goes Will Turner, producer to the stars, wait and see."

The two friends would say, "Sure you will," and laugh and say, "Don't forget us when you get there. In the meantime, you got two bucks so we can get some Cokes, big man."

Trolly opened his eyes and surveyed the walls of his studio surrounded by gold and platinum records. He had made it, yet his was a lonely life, and Val could change that for him.

He remembered his two friends. One had been shot in a corner fight and died in the street at age eighteen. His other best friend he had seen by chance a year or two ago on a street corner. Trolly had stopped his car, got out, and they hugged, hit fists, spoke for a few minutes and went their separate ways.

His only real friend was Dex, and he reached over and called him. "Yo, whatcha doing? Didn't wake you, did I?"

"No you fool, it's only 3:45 A.M. What the hell do you think I'm doing?"

"I can't find Val since I've been back. You think something's wrong?"

"Did you call her?"

"Lots of times, no answer. I'd go over but she begged me to cool it till she talked to Vince. Can I come over?"

"At 4:00 A.M.? You're getting nuts, but okay I'll put on some coffee."

"No, I'll get it at Dunkin Donuts and bring it. You still like black?"

"Yup, and plain donuts, not the jelly ones. See you soon."

Chapter Thirty-Two

Trolly hung up the phone receiver, turned back to the panel board, and replayed the new song he had just recorded. Placing a disc in his computer, he burned a copy to take to Dex and let him hear the rough cut. He finished and closed down his equipment, turned off the lights, and went to his car.

Trolly headed for the Dunkin Donut shop, which looked surprisingly crowded for that time of night, and decided to park across the street so as not to have a parking problem in the lot.

"Let me have a dozen assorted but no jelly and throw in a couple of plain and three chocolate," he said, pointing to the case containing the donuts.

"Anything else, sir?"

"Yes, two large coffees, one black and extra cream in the other."

"Cream is on the side counter, sir."

"Thanks, and keep the change," Trolly said as he handed the young server a twenty, smiled, and moved to the door.

"Thank you, sir. Have a good night, and please come again."

As Trolly crossed the wide street carrying a dozen donuts and a paper cardboard container with large coffees, he didn't see the dark car pull out and pick up speed until it was on top of him.

There was a loud thud as the impact crushed him into the fender, then his head broke the windshield, tossing him several feet away. He landed limp and motionless in the street.

"Get out of here."

"The fender or something is pressed up on the left wheel and I can't straighten the tire." Both men jumped out of the car, pulling on the fender and trying to lift it so the tire would be free. They pulled as one of the men caught his jacket on the fender and pulled it free. They jumped back in the car and quickly pulled away as some people ran from the shop toward the inert form of the guy on the ground.

The dark car, with visible front end damage, headed for the expressway and toward the airport.

"Take it to the scrap metal yard and the compactor. We need to get rid of this baby for good."

Taking out his cell phone, the driver called someone and said, "Meet us at the yard."

Several minutes later, they pulled into the yard where a night watchman let them drive in. As they got out of the car, one of the men said, "Make it look like a cereal box. Do it tonight and ship it out tomorrow, understand?" He handed the guy several hundred-dollar bills then turned to walk away. "We never want to see this baby recognizable again."

Several men appeared and took the car down a patch of ground and onto a conveyor belt.

"Yo, Mike, let me check it out and see if anything good is in there before you make it look like a matchbox." Sometimes a valuable camera or wallet was left in the car before it made its final destination.

"Find anything?" shouted the other workman.

"No nothing here...Wait a minute. Something is caught on the fender. A piece of torn material with I don't know, looks like a gold dice, but it does have a diamond. I got it. Start the crane." A large magnet on an overhead crane came down, crushed the car, and carried it aloft.

A car arrived, pulled in, turned off its headlights, a man got out and asked,

"You alright?"

Without an answer, the other two men got in the car and headed over the bridge back to New Jersey. Arriving at his home, one of the men entered by the back entrance, raced upstairs, and buzzed into the intercom. "Sammy back yet with the broad? Send her up as soon as they get here."

He quickly got out of his clothes and noticed his shirt sleeve was torn and one of his cufflinks was missing.

Dazed, Dex was awakened by the ringing of his bedroom phone. "Hello?"

"Mr. Randle please."

"Speaking. Who is this?"

"Mr. Randle sir, this is Officer Conners of the Accident Investigation Division. We found your card in the wallet of a Mr. Turner who has been injured in a hit-and-run accident."

Dex looked at the clock and saw it was 6:13 A.M., and he immediately realized he had fallen back asleep after Trolly's late call. "What did you say? Where? How is he? Is he okay?"

"Sir, he's at Drexel Medical Hospital, and he's badly injured. The investigation is ongoing, and we don't have too

175

much information. He was crossing a street with donuts and coffee and apparently didn't see the car that hit him and never slowed down."

"Thanks for calling. When can I get the A.I.D. report? Is it filed yet?"

"I don't have that information, sir."

Dex was trembling as Donna raised on one elbow and said, "What is it?"

"It's Trol. He's been hurt. I'm getting dressed, and I'll call you from the hospital."

"Should I come with you?"

"No, let me run. Love you. I'll call."

Forty minutes later, Dex entered the hospital and was informed his friend was in the intensive care unit and could not have visitors. The head nurse gave Dex some basic information, that Mr. Turner had been admitted around 4:30 A.M. with multiple injuries including head trauma, broken ribs, and a fractured leg.

Most serious was the head injury with swelling of the brain lining, which had to be lessened. Dex was told he should talk to the doctor in charge for any more information.

"Do you know of any family members we can contact?" the nurse asked.

Dex tried to think of Trolly's sister down south and promised to get that info for her.

"Where can I find his doctor?"

"He should be back on rounds within the hour."

Dex walked over to the coffee urn and poured a paper cup of black coffee and sat down to wait. If only Dex had not agreed to him getting coffee and donuts in the first place this would not have happened. He put the coffee down as if it was the beverage's fault and punished himself by not drinking from the cup.

Several minutes later, a gray-haired distinguished-looking man in a white coat with a stethoscope around his neck approached him and shook his hand. "Mr. Randle, I'm Dr. Cooper. I understand you're Mr. Turner's friend and attorney. Do you know any of his family members?"

"Nice to meet you, Doctor," Dex answered, "but not under these circumstances."

"I understand."

The doctor smiled. "We need to contact his family. He needs to lessen the pressure on his brain, and there is massive swelling and bleeding."

"There is a sister down south, but I have a power of attorney, and you need to do whatever you need to save him."

"We need to do it immediately."

"How bad is he?"

The doctor didn't answer, but his kind face showed the concern he felt. "We'll do everything possible, but you should contact his sister and tell her she might want to fly up as quickly as possible."

Dex called home. After telling Donna Trolly's condition, he asked her to call his office and tell his associate to see if the A.I.D report had been filed and to check his phone index to see if he had any info or numbers for Trolly's sister.

"Please call Val and tell her the news and, if possible, drive her down to the hospital," he said.

"I'm so sorry. What else should I do?"

"That's it for now. See you later. I'm going to hang here."

Chapter Thirty-Three

When Donna and Val arrived at the intensive care unit, they found Dex sitting in the waiting room aimlessly leafing through a magazine. Donna rushed over and kissed her husband on the cheek asking, "How is Trolly?"

Val nodded to Dex, slumped onto a chair next to the nurses' station, and stared into space. So much had happened and in such a short period of time. It was like a bad dream.

The confrontation with Carpozzi the night before, mixed with alcohol and sleeping pills, was exerting itself on her ability to express emotion, rather she seemed to be drifting in and out of reality.

She sat motionless on the chair, not even asking about Trolly or attempting to see him.

Dex, sensing her condition, got up and walked to her side, and suddenly a torrent of grief exploded and she cried uncontrollably as Dex hugged her.

While in this state, the doctor appeared and spoke in low tones to Dex. "Mr. Turner's condition has worsened. We can no longer wait to relieve the pressure on the brain. I need to operate and ease the pressure and check the blood from swelling the brain any further."

Dex nodded, and the doctor put his hand on Val and smiled slightly. "It will be okay."

"Thank you, Doctor," Val said almost in a whisper.

"We'll wait here for word."

"Mr. Randle, it will be a while. Why don't you all go get some breakfast?"

Downstairs in the hospital cafeteria, Val kept asking Dex about the accident and how it happened. Dex explained as much as he knew and let Donna stay with Val as he excused himself to make some calls. He called his office, and Sara told him several reporters had already called, as well as an Officer Conners who asked him to call back.

Dex called the number Sara had given him, and the phone was answered, "Police precinct, Sergeant Smith here."

"Yes, Officer Conners please."

There was a click and a voice responded, "Conners here."

"Good morning. This is Dex Randle returning your call."

"Sorry about your friend. I hope he's alright. I'd like to speak to you as soon as you can. I could drive to the hospital but your office might be better."

"Trolly is undergoing surgery. How about if I call you later when I know more about his condition, and I can drive to my office?"

"Talk to you later."

Dex returned to the cafeteria and sat down. Val was sobbing, and through the tears said, "It's my fault this happened." Donna tried to calm her.

"It's my fault. I didn't mean for anything to happen. I love him."

"What do you know?" Dex asked.

179

"Only that Vincent treated me horribly and I feared for Trol and me. He's really an evil man like you couldn't understand."

Dex got up, walked to another spot, and placed a call to Officer Conners.

Waiting in a hospital visitors' area is a study of human experience, watching the different ways people deal with the reality that someone they love faces mortality. That a doctor's words often can mean relief or cause a change in their lives forever.

Several hours later, the doctor appeared in the waiting room, still in his scrubs and surgical head scarf.

"Mr. Turner is in recovery, and we reduced the swelling but he's not out of danger. Recovery will take some time, and there could be residual damage."

Dex thought this doctor would not get an A in bedside manner. *Was it Trolly's condition that had caused the change in personality?* Dex thought. "Dr. Cooper, what does that mean in plain English?"

"Your friend has severe injuries and time will tell. Pray for his recovery."

"Thank you."

"I'll stop back later to check on him, but you should go home and get some rest. This will not be short term. I'm sorry."

Dex spoke to Donna, "Take Val back to our house. I've got to check with the police."

"Officer Conners, thanks for coming. Nice to meet you." Dex escorted the officer down the hall to his office. He liked the appearance of the man who had a short crew cut and square jaw line and looked as if he'd be good to have on your side in a brawl.

He took a seat opposite Dex without more than a nanosecond look around the office. Ignoring the platinum albums and collectibles most first-time visitors commented on, he expressed his sorrow about Trolly's injuries.

"I understand you and he go back a lot of years. Does he have any enemies you know of?"

"Why that question? Do you suspect something?"

"Mr. Randle, I appreciate your concern, but I would like you to answer the questions not raise new ones."

"Sorry, I guess that comes with the territory when you're a lawyer." Dex smiled but got no smile back.

"Actually Trolly—that's his nickname—is liked by everyone. He has few close friends, but no one really could have a problem with him...Wait, there is one person."

"And who would that be?"

"He and Vince Carpozzi sure don't like each other."

"That Vince Carpozzi?"

"Yes. Carpozzi owns a record company that Trolly produced some records for, and Trolly is engaged to Val Clifton. Carpozzi doesn't like that—"

"Don't know much about the music business should I know who Val Clifton is?"

"She has a double platinum album, and Carpozzi didn't appreciate Trolly's interference."

"Enough to try and kill him?"

"Enough."

"Fill me in, and don't spare the details."

"Don't know that much, other than he and Trolly were like oil and water."

"We have our own reasons for wanting to get information on Carpozzi, and it's been developing for quite some time, but I'm not at liberty to discuss."

Dex told him all he knew about the situation but didn't mention Val, Carpozzi, and his boxer client Don Carson and the Las Vegas fiasco. That was for another time. At the moment, he only wanted to get the people responsible for Trolly being near death.

Dex did learn there was possibly a dark-looking car, which some of the witnesses recalled seeing pull away, and the police were checking repair shops and also covering some chop shops for any leads, but so far nothing had turned up.

"Do you know what kind of car Carpozzi drives?" asked the officer.

"Mostly big limos and who knows what else? I think he had an English racing green SUV also." Conners made a notation in his notepad.

Dex thought this was like a movie. The square-jawed detective was jotting notes in a little spiral notepad.

Standing, the officer thanked Dex for his time and said, "I'll be in touch. Here's my card. If you think of anything, please call. I can find the way out."

After he was gone, Sara poked her head in and whispered, "Who is that hunk? He can arrest me anytime."

She took one look at Dex, saw his expression, and quickly returned to her desk.

Dex called patient info at the hospital and after a pause learned there was no change in Trolly's condition and that he was still critical.

He then called home, and Donna told him that Val had asked for a drink, took a pill, and was upstairs in the guest room. Dex put down the receiver and touched his stomach as an overwhelming pain and sick feeling took command.

Chapter Thirty-Four

With all the turmoil surrounding her and the life-threatening injury to Trolly, Val never mentioned the disc she had sent to Dex for safekeeping and he of course had no knowledge of it being in a pile of demos near his intern's desk.

The next several weeks settled into a pattern. After the initial shock of Trolly's accident, Val returned to her apartment. She was determined not to cause anymore trouble, and she missed her career and the attention it brought.

Her world as she knew it was on hold. The record company didn't call, Carpozzi was unreachable, and even Sammy her manager did not return calls. In effect, she was being frozen out by her team, and it was as if she didn't exist in the music world. Radio play on her album, without promotion money and support, had all but dried up and her once skyrocketing career was coming down faster than it had risen.

Val was living on sleeping pills, occasional drugs, and vodka. She was experiencing what many artists have endured, the collapse of a career after tasting success. There is nothing tougher or more depressing to an artist who has tasted fame, then to lose it. The world is full of so called one-hit-wonders who never reclaim their glory days and it's the ultimate insult to their life. Often in the solitude of her apartment, she would stare at her double platinum plaque hanging so proudly on her wall, and she would talk to it and tell it there would be more to join the wall and it would have company.

She visited Trolly every day. He was surviving while fighting for his life, but improvement was barely perceptible. She came every day and held his hand, and on occasion would sing to him, hoping it would cause a stirring and restore him to life. Several times when Dex would visit the hospital room he would find Val lying next to Trolly, holding his hand and singing *Come In Out of the Rain*, and it would near break his heart.

The investigation was proceeding at its own snail's pace, and not much had been discovered. When Dex called Officer Conners, there was little new information forthcoming.

"I'll let you know when we have something material to say. I did check out Carpozzi, but it seems he was at home all night—at least that's what two guys in the house said."

"Of course they would back him up," Dex said.

"He even had some singer stay the night with him and that also checks out though I didn't think I got the whole story from her."

"Thanks, but I just feel this was no accident. What about the car?"

"No trace, and no repair shops reported dark front-end damaged cars that night. Probably was chopped and shipped out or even could have been turned into junk scrap metal and shipped out, but nothing so far."

"What about Carpozzi and his cars?"

"Near as I can tell, he has a stable of cars but I couldn't find a dark green SUV. On questioning, he said he had one but it was a while back and that he got rid of it. I'm still checking."

"What about a witness? Somebody must know something?"

"Sorry. That's it for now."

Dex tried to keep his life in balance. He still had his family and busy practice but without the two or three calls a day from Trolly, there was a void, and the burning question of who did this and if Trolly would ever return to normal was never out of his thoughts. It was as if he was on autopilot.

The boys and Donna noticed a change in Dex who did his best to act normal around them, but there was a sadness and an unexplained loss of his usual upbeat and often childish charm that had kept him young and unpredictable. That spontaneity was missing.

Several times in the middle of a conversation the boys would have to repeat questions, and Dex would look up and try to reply, not knowing what they asked.

To Donna he would get even more philosophical, questioning life and how fragile it is, then asking what he could do for his friend. Secretly, Dex partly blamed himself for telling Trolly to come over at four in the morning, and he vowed never to eat another donut.

Most of all he was determined to avenge his friend, and he knew deep in his soul that it was no accident. Vincent Carpozzi had to be brought down, but how?

Chapter Thirty-Five

Vincent Carpozzi had skimmed some of the record company profits and used the proceeds to repay a large portion of the money wagered and lost on the football game.

The money was diverted by crediting against the actual sale of albums that had been returned as not sold by the distributor. This manipulation of charging returns instead of sales thus lowered profits and increased returned goods. A second set of books was used to keep these records for accounting purposes. It was the unreported profits that were then used to pay the gambling losses.

The events of the evening Trolly had been run down were never mentioned among his cronies. It was a non-issue that was better buried in the past. The question of what to do about Val and her singing career was not so easily disposed of, and much discussion ensued.

"Boss, I don't want to upset you but agents keep calling with gigs for her, and I don't know what to tell them. Are we keeping her on the label or what?"

"Sammy, let me do the thinking. She's not doing gigs, not recording, not doing press, not doing a damn thing, and she's lucky to be alive. That bitch is gonna pay and pay big, but we got to lay low for now, especially with the cops snooping around about the hit-and-run."

"Keep her supply of pills and drugs going. I wouldn't care if she overdosed, if you catch my drift."

Sammy looked at Carpozzi and nodded, staring ahead.

"I don't want you delivering them to her. Use one of the boys. Stay away from her until I tell you what I want done."

Sammy understood Carpozzi was not done with this matter.

It was nearing the end of the semester, and Dex was going to wrap up the lecture before finals with a summary of the entertainment law course. "So again think of the entertainer or athlete as a pie, and from that pie you take chunks or slices for the people surrounding the artist."

Dex drew a circle on the board and in one slice put an A for agent, another slice marked with an M for manager, and another with an L for lawyer. There were also slices for PR— public relations, an S for security, and a large slice with an R for record company. "It should be obvious that with all these slices coming from the artist's pie, only a small portion is left for the performer." Dex saw a hand shoot up and nodded to the student.

"Professor, so how do you protect the artist if such a large portion is taken?"

"That's the trick for good lawyers to protect the artist and make sure the slices given away are for work done for the artist and not given to lightweights who talk a good game and don't advance the artist's best interests.

"Also you make sure the portion that's left for the artist is worthwhile and that he gets his fair share and hopefully saves some of it after he pays taxes."

Dex almost wanted to use the Val's story as a working example of how things can go wrong in a promising career, but dared not for fear of violating the attorney-client privilege and saying too much on the subject.

"Any questions for the coming exam, remember it's all about spotting the issues. I don't care what you decide when answering an exam question, as long as you spot all the relevant issues and then explain your reasoning. I prefer shorter answers without a lot of BS, and for those who don't use laptops please write legibly so I can read your answers. Good luck in the future, and if you need recommendations to law firms for jobs, call me but only after the exams are in and marked."

The class gave Dex a round of applause, and he felt good as he left the podium. Another class would soon be graduating to face the real world to find that if they thought studying was tough, wait until they had to satisfy bosses, deal with ever-demanding clients, and pay back mounting student loans and do it all with a smile.

Dex left school and headed to the hospital to visit Trolly. He now knew all the nurses on the floor, and they would give him a brief update on Trolly's condition before he would go into his room. Almost always, he would find Val by the bedside keeping him company. Trolly was slowly improving, and at long last was now conscious and alert.

A side effect of the concussion and head injury was a ringing in his ears that never seemed to go away. The doctors called it a form of tinnitus, an inner ear problem that causes a ringing or sound that disturbs hearing. Trolly joked the ringing was like a rap beat, and if it kept humming in his ear he was going to produce the sound as a beat and copyright it.

"Probably would be a hit," Val joked.

They all tried to make light of the ringing, but if it did not go away it would destroy the perfect pitch Trolly was born with that enabled him to reproduce any sound musically. A producer couldn't produce records if he couldn't hear music in his head.

Dex had a power of attorney for his friend and was paying his bills and keeping things current, but the money supply was starting to dwindle, and in his condition, there was no business discussed, for fear, it would cause him additional stress.

Dex asked Val if he could drive her home. She looked like she had not eaten a decent meal in weeks, so he suggested she come home with him and have dinner and see Donna and the kids.

Once in the car and away from Trolly, Val broke down and between sobs told Dex much of the Carpozzi story, and how no one returned her calls and she was doing nothing all day. She was not so much looking for answers as just needing to let it all out, and Dex provided the release.

She actually seemed to be in better spirits when she entered the house and embraced Donna as they both disappeared into the kitchen. Dex walked into his den and his eyes caught his copy of *The Art of War* and he wondered how Sun Tzu would handle Carpozzi.

Chapter Thirty-Six

Several more weeks passed, and Val kept up her visits to Trolly who was steadily improving and, with the aid of a walker, was permitted to move freely about his room and the hospital corridor.

"I can remember most everything, but I can't seem to get this damn ringing sound out of my ears."

"The doctor thinks it will disappear with time, dear, so let's just concentrate on you getting better and coming home."

"I love you. Are you taking care of yourself? You look like you've lost weight, and you seem very nervous. What's going on out of this hospital room?"

Val had not mentioned she was being ignored by her manager and record company. Trolly was in no condition to be burdened with her problems, and she tried to be cheerful and hide her apprehension.

"It will be alright as soon as they let me out of here. I can take care of you, and we'll go back into the studio and come up with some great material."

"I know, so hurry up and get better." Val kissed him good-bye and moved toward the elevator.

Trolly watched as Val walked down the hall, then he turned and stood on one foot hoping the ringing in his ears would disappear. He remembered as a kid when you get water in your ear after swimming, standing on one foot and shaking from side to side.

Carpozzi paced in the record company office, walked over to his bar, and poured himself a scotch and water. The smooth scotch felt good going down but didn't quench the fire and rage that was building.

Sitting down, he pushed the intercom and said, "Get Sammy for me, will you? Tell him I want him now."

"Right away, Mr. Carpozzi."

"Yeah, boss, you want me?" Sammy said as he appeared within minutes.

"Sammy, I've got to go out to the west coast for a few days. While I'm away, maybe you should pay her a visit," he said, specifically not mentioning Val by name.

"I hear she takes a lot of pills and drugs, and maybe it would be nice if she had company."

Sammy started to say something but Carpozzi waved his hand and shut him off.

"I ain't no fool. I've noticed how you looked at her over the last year, and—"

"No, sir, I never touched her, boss."

"Sammy, listen to me. Maybe you should remember our last conversation. I'll be back at the end of the week." Carpozzi smiled at Sammy. "You have yourself a real nice week, and I do mean nice."

Carpozzi left the office, returning to his home, and he packed and called the LA office, telling them he wanted his staff to meet him in Vegas the day after next and to make the necessary plans. He took the evening flight to Vegas, and with the three-hour time difference, he was able to have a late dinner at the Mirage Hotel and Casino with two associates who had accompanied him on the flight.

After dinner, he returned to his hotel and went to the casino where he eyed the action, the lights and the noise, and found an empty space at the craps table where he requested and took out a $5000 marker.

When he got his chips, he put three black ones on the pass line and five behind the line. Placing the six and eight for $300 on each number, he watched a pretty blonde in a low-cut blouse blow on the dice and make the point, then hit numbers and passes as he increased his bets and stacked hundred-dollar and five-hundred-dollar chips in his rack.

A few more passes and numbers, and he had winnings of $20,000 or so in his rack.

"Here, doll, keep on rolling them numbers. This is for you," he said and tossed a five-hundred-dollar chip on the table for the roller.

She looked up and smiled at him, rubbed the dice suggestively on her chest, and rolled them, hitting the backboard and watching a six and five come up for a winning come out pass.

The people roared, and she said, "Thanks for the chip," and blew a kiss toward Carpozzi.

She pocketed $1000 and looked at him as he placed another chip on the line for her. She sevened out and lost the dice, ending her roll.

Carpozzi pushed his winning stack of chips to the stickman and said, "Color me up and cash me out."

"Thirty-one thousand, Mr. C."

Carpozzi tossed two five-hundred-dollar chips on the table for the dealers, who all thanked him and certainly would remember the tip, and started to walk toward the blonde.

"Thanks for the chip. Can I buy you a drink?"

"Why not, but let's have it in my suite."

As they headed for the elevator, Carpozzi smiled and thought, *Life ain't bad at all,* as he put his arm around the blonde. "What did you say your name is?"

Carpozzi had been right about Sammy, who over the months had been hungry for Val. He often thought she needed to be taught a lesson and he could really teach her plenty. Sammy called her to set up a meeting, one she would never forget. He walked into the bathroom and laughed to himself. He was hard just thinking about her and the meeting.

Chapter Thirty-Seven

Val had spent the day visiting Trolly and upon arriving home took off her clothes, poured herself a glass of wine, and was running a bath when the phone rang.

"Hello. Sammy is that you?" she asked when she heard the voice at the other end of the phone.

"Sorry I haven't gotten to you sooner, but there were complications—"

Val interrupted, "It's okay. I understand, but it's been terrible what with the accident and no one from the company even calling me. What's happening?" There was a momentary silence on the phone and she continued speaking. "How's Vince? Is he still furious at me?"

"I think it can all be worked out. Should I come over and we can talk?"

Val hesitated but thought this was possibly her only chance to get her career restarted. "Yes, of course. When do you want to come?"

"How about in a couple of hours? You take it easy, and I'll be there around nine."

"Maybe I'll bring you a treat. How's your supply?"

"Sammy. I'm clean. I don't need anything."

"Great. See you then."

Val stretched out in the tub, and her thoughts turned to how she could convince Sammy she was ready to sing again and tour. Carefully applying her lipstick, she took her clothes from the closet, wanting to look great but not too sexy so he wouldn't get any ideas. Finally, settling on a simple but form-fitting blouse and jeans she unbuttoned her top two buttons—not enough to see but just enough to want to look. She felt very casual but very put together. She had one more glass of wine to settle her down, and she awaited her meeting.

Music, that's what I need, she thought. Placing her own CD in her player, she lowered the volume so it would be heard but not obvious. Val then decided she should have a snack or something available for Sammy, and she tried to remember what he liked. She had been in his company for around 18 months, many times for dinner and meals together while on the road, yet she realized she couldn't even say what he liked. She was embarrassed by her lack of knowing anything about him. Always taking him for granted, he suddenly was her only link to Carpozzi and getting her career moving again.

She awaited his arrival and turned on the TV to kill some time, but her nerves were taking hold of her so she got up, went into the kitchen, and decided to make some dip and cut up some cheese and slice carrots and celery and placed them on a tray with assorted crackers.

She thought about one more glass of wine but she decided she had enough and instead took half a Valium to help calm down.

Finally the doorbell rang and she took one last glance in the mirror, tossed her hair, and opened the door. Sammy entered and had a bottle of red wine and a package, which he placed on the table.

"You look great, and how are you?"

"Just fine. So do you. Looks like you lost some weight." Val wanted to kick herself for that comment but Sammy didn't seem to notice.

"Please sit down. Can I get you a drink? How about some cheese and crackers?" Val asked nervously.

"Thanks. I'll open this bottle. So tell me, how you making out? How's your producer friend doing?"

"He's coming along, but it's really slow progress."

"Yeah, terrible thing. I hope they catch them bastards."

"How's Vincent?"

"He's fine. He's out in Vegas this week checking out some talent if you know what I mean."

Val understood and nodded. This conversation was going nowhere and both felt stilted, but Val sensed a different attitude from Sammy. He no longer regarded her as off limits. She was no longer the boss's exclusive property.

Val shifted uncomfortably in her chair and almost automatically buttoned one of the buttons on her blouse. She decided to join Sammy in having a drink. As he poured it, he opened the package and out tumbled a plastic bag of white powder.

"Thought you might want some of this. It's really good stuff." Sammy poked a hole with his penknife in the bag, and he carefully arranged two lines of the powder on a little dish and handed it to Val who took the dish, bent down, and sniffed the line while wiping the excess powder along her gums. There was an almost instant hot flash, and she could feel her heart beating rapidly.

"So I guess you want to get started recording again or even playing some gigs."

"Sammy, I do, I do. Can you help?"

"Vince is really pissed at you, but maybe I could talk to him and convince him it would be good for all, but I don't really know."

Sammy was staring at her, taking in every inch of her body and savoring her breathing, which was more pronounced, causing her breasts to expand and push up against the thin material of her blouse.

"Would you like a refill?" Val asked, hoping to break the tension. She stood and bent slightly to pour the drink but spilled the wine.

The drinks, Valium, and coke caused her to stumble, and she brushed against Sammy.

"I can help you, but you've got to help me." Val pulled back but his grip tightened.

He roughly touched her blouse, and with one motion of his large hand, the buttons flew open exposing two round white pieces of art with jutting nipples that waited for his tongue. The rage and desire were beyond longing. They were to be satisfied, and his hunger caused her very touch to set his body on fire.

Val pulled back to resist, but his other hand circled her waist and drew her against him, setting his heart pumping and his nerve endings tingling. He had been waiting for this moment for months, and there was no Carpozzi, no Trolly, and no crowds to stop him. There was only Val and his needs and nothing but for him to be satisfied.

"Sammy, please no, no, stop," she said, trying to pull away and only increased his roughness and desire.

He explored with his hands and ripped at her pants. She escaped his grasp for a moment, but he was too strong, and as his weight settled on her he slapped her under her right eye, which swelled immediately.

Gripping her with both hands, he yanked her around as his hand moved below her, and he bent her over and penetrated her with surprising ease. Her wetness caught him off guard. "Hey, girl, you liking this?"

She whimpered and begged him to get off, which excited him even more. He grabbed one of her breasts and squeezed her nipple as she cried out in pain, but at the same time she was getting excited, and she hated herself for even thinking that was possible.

Val understood she was now fighting for her life, and even under the daze of drugs knew she had to buy some time for her survival. Resistance would be to no avail, so Val turned her head back to meet his face and said, "Slow down so we can both enjoy this." She licked his ear.

"You like this, don't you, baby? You're not used to a real man. Come here." He brought her to his lap and forced her to move in and out.

His largeness forced Val to cry in pain, and Sammy into pushed her even faster, causing the friction to make him swell up in her.

Val had to survive this ordeal if only for Trolly's sake because he really needed her, and she thought if Sammy was satisfied, perhaps she could escape.

He was breathing fast and whispering, "You need this." He twisted her almost as if she was weightless to place her face on his penis and forcing the back of her head to move with her mouth, covering him.

She gasped for breath, but he held her against him, and for the first time her hands were free. He let out a loud gasp and exploded with force as her face and body became covered with his manhood.

Val leaned back as he momentarily let go, and she saw the fruit and cheese dish when he grabbed her, twisting her onto the table and into the mound of white powder.

He forced her face down in a rage and screamed, "Bitch, snort it."

Val held her breath and while covered in the approaching death, she inched her free hand across the table and found the knife she had used to cut the carrots.

"You ain't so big now, are you? Beg for your life, 'cause that platinum album don't mean shit now, baby."

She attempted to turn her head away from the powder as he hit her on the side of her back, and she thought she would black out from the pain. She closed her fingers on the knife handle, and as he pushed her back into the white powder she crossed her hand in a wide arch, striking Sammy in the neck.

He looked up as if in disbelief. "You bitch," he said and paused, gasping for air as blood poured from his neck and mouth. He made a gagging sound, and he lurched forward, his eyes still open and his weight pinned Val beneath him. She lay there for a moment and attempted to slide out from under him, and she fell to the floor too exhausted to move.

Sammy was face down in the powder and across the table.

Val caught her breath, wiped her hand mixed with coke and blood, and started to cry. Leaning against the table and not touching Sammy, she stumbled to the phone.

She thought about calling 911 but stopped and rang a number.

"Dex, it's Val. I've been raped, and Sammy is dead. Help me."

"What? Where are you? Don't touch anything."

"My apartment. Come quick."

"Val, listen to me. Don't do anything. Don't take a shower or clean yourself. Don't say anything to anybody till I get there, I'm on my way."

Twenty-five minutes later, Dex opened the door to the apartment and found Val bloody and naked slumped in a corner. Sammy was face down covered in white powder stained by his blood, the knife still in his neck.

Dex gently covered Val in her robe and placed two calls. The first to Officer Conners who said he'd be right over and the second to 911 telling them to send an ambulance. He tried to comfort Val as she broke down only saying, "He raped me, and I stabbed him."

Chapter Thirty-Eight

Dex tried to reassure Val everything would turn out okay and to say only that Sammy had sexually assaulted her and then tried to smother her in the cocaine.

Val sobbed and was almost in a state of shock when the police and ambulance arrived. The EMS quickly assessed the situation, gave her an intravenous drip, placed her on a gurney, and were about to transport her to the hospital.

She was leaving as Officer Conners arrived with another individual who identified himself as an agent with the FBI.

Seeing Dex, they walked over, and Dex told them what he had recounted earlier to the police.

Conners was taking notes and looked up to ask, "Was Miss Clifton on drugs?"

Dex answered that as far as he knew she wasn't a regular user.

"What was her relationship to the deceased?" asked the other individual.

"He acted as her manager."

The FBI guy turned to Conners. "Wasn't he working for Carpozzi?"

Conners looked him off as if to say don't talk too much.

"Hey, how come the FBI is here?" Dex asked.

The question was ignored.

Another question popped into Dex's mind, but he didn't ask, why Conners was with an FBI agent and why he seemed at ease telling the agent to cool it.

The police had cordoned off the entrance to the apartment and were taking pictures of everything in sight and had drawn an outline in chalk as to where Sammy had been.

A young assistant district attorney arrived, ducked under the tape and made his way toward Conners when he spotted Dex. "Hi, Professor Randle. How are you?"

Dex recognized him as a former student from his law course and said hello, but couldn't remember his name.

Dex thought, *Police, FBI and the DA's office, what next?* He didn't have long to wait to get an answer as two local reporters appeared from TV stations and immediately sought out Officer Conners.

Dex began to understand that Conners was more than just an Accident Investigation Division officer as he had been originally led to believe when he was questioned about the hit-and-run. Who was this guy and why was he everywhere?

The evening news played up the story with Val being raped and in the hospital.

Of course, the interviews had the mandatory sound bites with the celebrity and record industry people injecting how horrified they were and what a great talent Val was and each would end with how close they were to her and how they were praying for her recovery.

Another station was doing interviews with women's rights groups who were already doing placards and posters on behalf of a woman's right to defend herself.

As word spread, it was becoming the lead story, and programs were interrupting normal broadcasts to tell viewers to stay tuned in for the latest breaking news.

DJs were replaying her album and their favorite cuts as they embellished the story.

Val, unaware of what was happening, was thrust back into the glare of celebrity. Sad but true how sick society is, and now Val was getting publicity and exposure she could never buy.

The DA and chief of police held a press conference in front of the hospital saying this was an ongoing investigation and there would be a careful but complete look into all the evidence before any determinations were made.

"Mr. Carpozzi, been trying to get hold of you, but your phone didn't answer." said an associate who while in his suite had seen the news flash on television. "We got a serious problem. Sammy is dead, and the story is he raped Val and tried to kill her. No, of course I'm serious, and the news is everywhere. You need to do something."

"Get a hold of the company's lawyers, and I'll call my personal attorney. Also, get our PR lady to draft something and have the lawyers review it. Arrange for my car to meet me at the airport. I'll be on the next flight out of here."

Carpozzi thought to himself, *Fuck. I'll have to make up with Val. It's best to give her some royalties until this blows over. What an idiot? How could Sammy get me into this jam?*

At the hospital, Val was examined, samples were taken, and she was then sedated after receiving four stitches under her right eye. She was also bandaged for a broken rib. The examination revealed much of what Val had said and the brutality of the attack. Photos of her cuts and bruises were recorded, both in color and black and white.

At the offices of Can't Take It with You Records, a group of attorneys was busy pontificating legal theories and potential lawsuits and what should be done when Carpozzi's personal attorney told everyone to shut up and listen.

"Here's the game plan. Sammy was not technically an employee of the company. He was her manager, employed and paid by her, and though we have no responsibility for his totally outrageous behavior, we feel a moral duty to stand by our recording artist, and we intend to be here for her and see her through these difficult times."

Looking at the public relations person, he continued, "Draft a response for Mr. Carpozzi as head of the company, but I don't want him on camera. Either you do it or get a damage control spokesperson to handle all of our responses. Nothing is done without my approval first. Also, send three dozen roses to Val's hospital room."

"What about Sammy?" a young lawyer asked.

"What about him?" replied the senior advocate. "He's not our problem. He's dead, and Mr. Carpozzi makes no statements of any kind, you all understand? I'm on my way to meet him at the airport before he says anything. No one says anything."

Dex, who by now felt he was getting to know Officer Conners, took out the card and private number he had been given by the officer. He hesitated for a moment and dialed his number.

"Officer Conners, it's Dex. You wanted me to call, but I need some answers from you first."

"Dex, really sorry about what happened tonight, and call me Jack. You available for some coffee? Let's meet at the midtown diner in say a half hour?"

"Okay, but you've got to come clean with me if you want my help, or I'm gonna play the attorney's game and say nothing until I have to."

"Fair enough. See you soon."

Dex entered the diner and spotted Conners in a far booth dressed in civvies and took notice of how different he looked when not in uniform. He seemed younger.

"Hey, how ya doing?"

Dex nodded and slid into the booth. "Who are you really, and why the FBI?"

"What we say here stays between us, you agree?"

"Yes."

"I'm working undercover with a joint task force made up of local police and the feds trying to bust a large group of people spread over a number of states for everything including racketeering, gambling, payoffs, blackmail, and murder. It includes Carpozzi, and we know there are links to your friend Trolly and his so-called accident. Looks like tonight is somehow also involved.

"We suspect you know more than you're saying. You're clean so far, but somehow Trolly, Val, and the record industry are all involved. Also rumors about some other of your clients keep popping up."

"What are you talking about? Who?"

"Let it go for now, but we really need to get some real answers. I need some cooperation, and assuming the investigation shows Val's self-defense claim is real, everyone would appreciate her help in answering some questions."

Dex met Conners' stare head-on, trying to figure out if he was suggesting in return for her testimony she would be cleared or if he was bluffing. Val had indeed acted in self-defense.

Dex didn't answer but asked, "Jack, what is needed for now?"

"Finish your coffee, and we'll talk again." He threw a five-dollar bill on the table, got up, and left.

Dex looked at him as he departed, took a sip of coffee, and tried to remember back to his early law school training and decided his two courses in criminal law were no match for all that was going down.

Carpozzi, tired from the red-eye flight from Vegas, was met at the airport outside of the terminal by his attorney, and in the limo he got a complete rundown of the news and actions taking place.

"So Mr. Carpozzi, we think it best you not appear, and a statement about your support of Val and your deep surprise and anger at this terrible occurrence will be given to the press. For now just let things play themselves out."

"What an idiot? How could he do such a thing?"

"You are correct, and of course my sympathy will be extended to Val, and Can't Take It with You Records will help her."

"Counsel, anything else I should do or know?"

"There is one additional piece of information I received from a source that it was more than just the local police at the scene tonight—there were some feds as well. Any reason or is there something I should know? If I'm to really help, I've got to know what is going on. Now is not the time for me to be surprised."

Carpozzi looked out the limo window and replied, "Not that I can think of, and thanks for coming tonight."

After arriving home, undressing, and getting a drink, a very tired and troubled Carpozzi went into his office, turned on his computer, and pulled up the record costs and expense sheet on Val's album. Making several adjustments to the statement, he then turned to the receipts section, made several notations, and turned off his computer. The next day was just another one in the life of Vince Carpozzi.

Chapter Thirty-Nine

There are many who believe that one's life can be forever altered and changed by four or five decisions that can occur by just luck or happenstance. A down and out person with just a couple of bucks in his pocket can turn down a street to buy a pack of cigarettes and look up and on impulse buy a winning lottery ticket that changes his life forever, because he ran out of cigarettes at that precise moment. A blind date you don't want to go on but are forced into by friend can turn out to be the find of your life who you end up marrying all because you happened to be free that night. You bump into a long lost friend who mentions a job opportunity just as you had been laid off. Each of these twists and turns can alter your life. Some call it destiny, others fate and still others divine intervention. Doesn't matter what it's called, only that it is what it is. Val, battered and shaken, lay in the hospital unaware her life was once again turning and spinning in a new direction. She had arisen from the ashes and was once again in the limelight. Groups of women were protecting her and making her their cause célèbre. Who could argue with a woman's right to defend herself?

Talk show hosts were competing to have her exclusive interview.

Four motion picture producers had calls into Dex's office, one even suggesting that when she felt well enough, who better than she to play the lead in her own story?

Three literary agents called to pitch her life story for book rights, and one guy even called to try to get her licensing rights for a self-defense video.

"Get attacked, ward off the attacker, and you are on the road to fame and glory," Dex said almost as an afterthought to Sara who had just handed him a fax from some gossip magazine asking for confirmation Val was pregnant by her attacker.

What could not be denied was this was one of those altering changes in her life. Despite her cuts and broken ribs, Val was remarkably composed when Dex and Donna visited her a couple of days later.

The police had been visibly absent after the initial interviews, and the DA would only say the investigation was ongoing and gave no further details. The hospital reports confirmed all she said took place. Dex told her to rest and he would explain to Trolly what had occurred.

Dex had discussed the events with Trolly, explaining Val had defended herself from Sammy and he had died in the incident, not mentioning the severity of the attack but only that Val was fine but had a broken rib, which had to be x rayed and bandaged, but she was otherwise well.

"When will I see her?" Trolly asked.

"She's at home resting under sedation, and I'll bring her in to see you this week. She said to tell you she loves you and even wanted me to give you a kiss for her, but I told her that was asking too much."

"You being straight with me?"

"Hey, man, do I lie?"

"Sammy's really dead? Couldn't happen to a nicer guy."

"Get some rest and get better soon."

"Dex, you aren't playing me, are you?"

"Get some rest. It's gonna be okay."

"What about my hit-and-run?"

"Police are still working on it and following some leads."

A few days later Dex received two separate letters in the mail, one was a royalty statement and check for Val and the second was a producer statement and check for Trolly.

Each was a statement of record sales to the end of the current period with a breakdown of advances expenses for cost of producing and recording the album, charges for pressing and manufacturing, half of certain promotion expenses, half the cost of the video and then a 'hold back' of twenty percent reserve against future returns from record stores. As Dex reviewed the total cost and expenses charged against the reported sales of the album, he was getting angrier and angrier. What initially looked like a royalty of close to $1 million plus, when all the charges were totaled, they amounted to $800,000 and some dollars, leaving a balance of approximately $200,000 and the holdback of twenty percent, leaving a check for $180,000. Dex guessed it was probably only about twenty-five percent of what Val really should have received.

Trolly's statement had many charges as well, and since his royalty rate was that of a producer, it was about a third of Val's check or around $60,000. He would have to deal with this, but this was not the right week.

It was days such as this that Dex thought he should be a full-time professor, and it caused him to think of his best pal Assistant Dean Hall. He picked up the phone and smiled as a familiar voice said, "Hello."

"Yo, Jerry, how ya doing?"

"Dex, what the hell is going on back in Philly? You alright? Even the papers out here are full of stories. What's with Trolly? And what are you doing in this Val mess? You don't know diddly about criminal law. Get some help."

Dex loved Jerry, and he had a way of coming right to the point. "You're right. I'm not really handling the case, but was trying to help Val, and it doesn't look like she will be charged with anything"

"At least for now you mean."

"Trolly is starting to feel better, but he has a ringing in the ear, and it could affect his career, but it's early yet, and the doctor is hopeful. What's with you?"

"Dex, I know you got a plateful of stuff happening, but all is well with me. In fact, keep your fingers crossed. The board is meeting next month."

"Really?"

"The dean is leaving, and he told me he suggested me as his replacement. They will do a nationwide search, but I'm told I'm the front-runner."

"Great. Couldn't pick a better dean."

"Thanks. How's Donna and the kids? When you coming down?"

"Little busy these days but great speaking with you. Take care."

"You take care, and don't take those crazy risks you do. This is not law school or a martial arts tournament. I'm not around to bail you out or cover your ass."

Thirty assorted men sat around at computers, some on the phones, and others at their desks, reading files while others passed information back and forth. A group of five stood in front of a chalkboard while Conners deftly compiled lists of pieces of evidence in three columns, with arrows all pointing in one direction toward one name. "Gentlemen, this is our target, and this is who we go after, then it will all crumble."

One of the men interjected, "Jack, but so far we got nothing on Carpozzi."

"We will, we will, and I know just where it will come from."

Chapter Forty

Dex stood at the podium and looked out at his class. To begin the first class of a new semester, he would survey the students and try to pick which student would be most interested in entertainment and sports law. Usually the first ten or so minutes were set aside for anything the students wanted to talk about. They would ask questions about what was current in the news, and that day was no exception.

Before Dex had even opened his notes, hands were raised and the first question asked. "Professor, are you going to tell us about all the newspaper articles regarding Val Clifton, and what about that hit-and-run?"

"Can't answer a lot of your questions because of attorney-client relationship and speak too much about what's going on. I can say that Val is improving as is Trolly, her producer. As you see on the news the police are investigating the matter and hopefully they will catch the people who hit Trolly."

"What about the death of that guy? I don't remember his name but he was her manager or something."

"That's under police review, but it looks like self-defense. The more interesting question and one you guys should understand—in fact it would be a good exam question," Dex hesitated and as if on cue the very mention of exam question got everyone ready to take down every word about to be said.

"Remember this for later in the semester, when we study record contracts and discuss advances and royalties. Let me pose this hypothetical set of facts. Suppose you represent an artist who entered a recording contract with a company and the first album when released sold about 1.2 million copies. What would the royalty statement look like, and how much would the artist get in her check?"

Dex looked at the young man who was about to speak and smiled, since he was the one that looked most interested in the course.

"Professor, we would need more facts, but assuming she got an advance, we would have to deduct certain expenses, from the royalties and she would get the balance."

"So what do you think an artist who goes platinum should receive?"

"Probably about four or five hundred thousand."

A second student said, "More like six or seven."

"Watch this." Dex turned to the board and started to write out a column of figures and words next to them. "Let's say she got a $100,000 artist advance on signing, which was paid to her, and the all in expense to produce the album, including the producer was another $300,000. Now add $100,000 more for promotion expense and another $150,000 for her share of the cost of the video plus cost of pressing, manufacturing, distribution, and artwork for the million-plus albums was another $250,000, so we now are up to $900,000 and if the royalty, just to keep the math simple was one dollar on each album sold we start at the top of the column with $1,200,000 deduct the $900,000, which leaves a balance of $300,000. We deduct a reserve against royalties, which record companies hold back to be paid over three accounting periods is $240,000, the check could look like $60,000 to $100,000.

"Imagine the look on your client's face when she thinks she's a millionaire and she ends up with a paltry hundred thousand. Now don't forget to give Uncle Sam his tax bite with state and local taxes, which could add up close to forty percent. She is now down to $60,000, and don't forget the manager cut of twenty percent, so she's down to $48,000, and the poor lawyer if he only gets $15,000, she has $25,000."

"Wow, that's a mouthful, and you probably didn't add in everything," one of the students blurted.

"I exaggerated for effect, but you get the picture. Now let's turn to the assigned cases for today."

The street guys assigned to the task force were turning up the pressure on the day-to-day activities of the local criminal element. Applying pressure would get them some info about who did what to whom.

Police, when trying to get info on a particular crime can often put pressure on the neighborhoods so as to get some piece of information in exchange for easing the heat. Maybe, just maybe, they could open a lead on the hit-and-run or what the word on the street was about the Val incident.

Several police had their own particular methods of getting sources of information—scaring a guy, promising to leave him alone to conduct his business, or cutting a deal for lesser charges in return for good and timely info. The more the pressure, the more certain something would break but no real info or leads were forthcoming.

Life does have its share of tricks, and just by chance, one of the officers caught a drug deal going down, and as he

216

handcuffed one of the guys who had a prior record and could not afford to get convicted again even for a minor drug charge, the guy said, "Listen, you interested in that hit-and-run? I think I got something of interest."

"I'm listening. What you got?"

"No way, man. This is hot stuff. You interested?"

"Depends. I'm all ears."

"If it's of interest, I walk?"

"It better be real good, punk, or you get double time."

"Could be you guys searching for a car. Well I could know something of interest, if I could jog my memory."

Thirty minutes later sitting in a small room with a cigarette, hot coffee, and Officer Conners, a story was unfolding about a compressed SUV at a steel compactor, and the real piece of info was there might be a clue that could have been found that never got compacted if a deal on the present charges was dropped.

"So my buddy operating the big crane asks me if I found anything in the truck before it compresses. I say no, but I'm looking at a big diamond, set in a cufflink, which looks like dice, which of course is now missing, but if my charges are dropped might be found."

"You playing us and you might go away for so long you'll forget what the sun looks like," Conners bellowed. "You'll need a walker just to go to the bathroom if this isn't real."

"Maybe we can work something out?"

"It's at a pawn shop and is still there. There's no real call for one cufflink, but the diamonds have real value."

Three patrol cars with sirens blaring and bright lights descended on the pawn shop, and when they were done with him, the owner felt it was his civic duty to turn over the cufflink.

The crew knew it was a break in the case, but had no idea who was the owner of the cufflink's mate.

Chapter Forty-One

Val was improving physically with each passing day, but there were disturbing signs of how much the attack and stabbing had really affected her.

Donna, who had developed a true affection for her, was now visiting her daily, and Val was unable to shake the trauma. Interviews were out of the question both from a legal point of view and even more so in that she was mentally not stable enough to be interviewed without breaking into hysteria. The doctors believed this would subside with time, but in the meantime, she was undergoing psychiatric sessions.

The longer she remained secluded, the greater the public clamor for details of the attack. How the public likes and thrives on bad news should be evident by the first 15 minutes of the evening news. Crime, fires and scandal are what bring ratings, and ratings bring advertisers, and advertisers bring money. Dex had really become the point man for news on the medical condition of both Trolly and Val, and tried to avoid the hordes of reporters who continually sought a scoop or something to satisfy their editors or news directors.

The record company tried to keep pumping the sales of the album, but Carpozzi, on advice of his attorney, kept a very low profile and avoided all contact with the press.

Since there was no available news on the subject, the next level of interest was the talking heads who conjured up points of interest, sometimes without proper foundations and could have an hour show talking up the propositions. Always the gossip and scandal sheets add fuel to the fire and then stroke it even higher by getting an alleged witness to swear to have witnessed some bizarre scene. Such was this very exciting and unsolved mystery that had the public begging for more and the press trying to provide them with answers.

The police, though not wishing to add to the excitement, nevertheless did also want to find the truth and ultimately to prove Carpozzi and others were acting in concert and conducting corrupt business and criminal activities. Conners had a detail of men trying to track the make of the car, who it belonged to and where it was located.

Another team was busy tracking jewelry stores and manufacturers trying to trace the cufflink and its owner. Officer Conners, acting on a hunch, called Dex.

"Dex, Jack Conners here. How you doing?"

"Fine. Kind of busy right now. What's on your mind?"

"Sorry to disturb you, but I thought we could talk for a few minutes. Mind if I come over to the office?"

"How about the diner? People get nervous on the floor if police come into a law office, bad for business."

"Okay. How about an hour?"

"Could you make it two? I have a musician coming in for a meeting regarding a song he says he wrote, which somebody recorded and he didn't get paid."

"Fine."

At the meeting with the client, a first-time music writer, he stated he was the sole author of a mega-hit single that someone recorded without his consent but had no copyright filed on the song, no demo, and never really had contact with the artist who recorded it. Dex told him to try to get some evidence and call him back when he did. If there was really no access to the alleged song, just because there were similarities in the sound, didn't mean somebody stole it.

Dex ran toward the elevator and called back to Sara that he would be back in an hour.

"Where you going to be?" Sara yelled back.

"Out."

Sara just looked up, shook her head and thought. Things sure were different. Everyone was so tense and the professor was very mysterious. No longer was this the fun practice she had envisioned when she first started interning.

"Dex, good to see you." Conners extended his hand. "How's Val doing and Trolly?"

"It's coming but slow. Val really has been through a great deal, and she's having trouble getting back to normal."

"I understand, and that Sammy was a brutal guy. Do you think he had anything to do with the hit-and-run?"

"Don't know, but nothing would surprise me."

"How about Carpozzi? Think he's involved?"

Dex nodded. "What are you thinking?"

"Hey, you don't wear cufflinks on your shirts, do you?"

"Rarely, except for formal when I wear a tux. Why, you need to borrow something?"

"No. I'd like to show you something and see if it registers."

Conners pulled a small plastic bag from his uniform pocket, opened it, and showed a diamond cufflink shaped like a dice.

"Where did you get that?"

Conners thought he caught an instant reaction from Dex. "Not important at this moment, but you ever see anything like it or a matching mate?"

Dex remembered the fights at Vegas, the record parties, and several newspaper photos. Trying to keep his best poker face, and remembering his martial arts training of showing no emotion he again asked, "Where did you find it, and why am I being shown the link?"

Conners sensed at once Dex identified the link and said, "Okay, but not a word of this gets out, agreed?" Dex nodded. "We arrested a small-time punk, and he offered this in exchange for cutting him a break. He said he found it in a car, which he thinks was a dark SUV. It was compacted and disappeared shortly after the hit-and-run. Now what do you know?"

"You're gonna love this, but I've seen these cufflinks on only one person, Vince Carpozzi."

"Get out. Don't kid me. Where? When? Give me details."

"Vince is a sharp dresser, and he wears them all the time. Haven't you ever noticed?" Looking at the way Conners dressed, he added, "Guess not."

"Let's keep this between us for the time being. Dex, you okay?"

Dex didn't answer, but his expression did.

"I mean no one is putting the squeeze on you, are they?"

"No, I'm fine. I do worry about Trolly and Val."

"I've been meaning to talk to you or Val when she's able 'cause I think she knows a lot more than she lets on. She has a past with Vince, and we believe she's involved in some prior doings with him."

"I wish you guys would let up on them."

"As soon as she's able, I really need to question her, and her cooperation would go a long way to help her, if you get my meaning. If you think she needs police protection, let me know. Take care. I'll be in touch, and thanks for your help."

Chapter Forty-Two

Dex decided to visit Trolly in the hospital, and on the way, replayed in his mind the conversation that had just taken place. A series of questions remained unanswered.

Would Carpozzi really be that stupid to attempt to kill Trolly himself? Why wouldn't he get someone else to do the dirty work? What was the connection between Sammy's actions and the car attack? What did Conners mean about the Carpozzi and Val connection? What else did Conners know?

The questions kept coming, and Dex was determined to start getting some answers.

Why did Conners even ask him about his owning cufflinks? Surely he wasn't a suspect, was he?

Would the cufflink tie Carpozzi to the hit-and-run? Was it sufficient evidence?

Many questions, few answers.

Entering Trolly's hospital room, he found it unoccupied and was surprised to learn that Trolly, IV still inserted in his arm was two floors below visiting Val for the first time since the attack.

When Dex arrived at Val's room, he found the two lovers holding hands, with Trolly in a chair pushed up against the hospital bed and Val saying, "I must look a mess."

"You look incredible to me, and I missed you so much. I'll never ever leave you again."

Tears were in Val's eyes, and she happened to look up as Dex entered the room, and she burst into tears.

All three had tears flowing and finally Dex said, "We all need to talk. You guys get better, but the police need to know everything."

"What can we tell them that they don't already know?" Trolly asked.

Val looked straight ahead but didn't say a word.

"They will be speaking to each of you."

"What about, we're the victims and they should arrest the people responsible." Val was too upset to talk to, and Dex reassured her all would be right and it was important she and Trolly just got better.

Dex mentally kicked himself for bringing up the police when it was the first time they had been together. "I'll let you two be alone and stop by tomorrow."

When Conners arrived at headquarters, he immediately assigned a desk clerk to find all the articles and pictures of Carpozzi that had been published in the past year.

"I want every picture you can find—baby pictures, anything, do whatever it takes."

Going to the chalkboard, he drew an arrow from the word *cufflinks* to the name Carpozzi. More and more of the arrows connected to this guy, and Conners was determined to get them all connected and bring this guy and his connections down.

"Hey Ron, take this picture and check out the better jewelry stores in Philadelphia and New Jersey. I want to know who bought these cufflinks. Also check with the feds and let them see it and have their guys do likewise in Vegas. Ask them to especially check the casino stores. They sell lots of expensive jewelry to high rollers."

Conners was barking out orders and it was apparent he was in command or at least high on the pecking order of this unit. "Karl, I want to find out everything about this scrap yard and car compressor company. Who owns it, and who delivers cars to them? Find out where the compressed cars end up. Nancy, get me all the history and background on Dex Randle, Val Clifton, and Will Turner. Find out how far back Val and Carpozzi go and what you can about them."

"Right, boss."

"Never call me boss while we are on this assignment, remember. How did Trolly and Val hook up? Do a background check on Val—where she came from, her family, anything that can shed some light on this trio."

"How deep you want us to go?"

"Deep enough to dig to China and back if it helps. When you find out about Val's family, fly out and interview them."

Conners speaking to no one in particular said, "Something isn't right here, so put up the pot of coffee and don't rest till we get some answers."

Many criminal defense lawyers have told their clients that when the local and federal authorities combine and decide to go after someone, that with all the tools and money they have in their arsenal, they are formidable opponents. Relentless in their pursuit and Conners could lead the pack. Many have learned that to be all too true.

Carpozzi and his connections were clearly in the sights of this unit, but no trigger could be pulled and no warrants served until they had a tight enough case and so far, they had hunches and bits and pieces. Slowly, it was coming together and Conners knew he was close to something big. Conners walked down a hall and into a sparse office where a leather-faced guy looked up with eyes that had shared and seen many, many experiences. His tight features belied his age, but it was evident he had earned and expected respect.

"Chief, it's moving along, and I'd like to get some wiretaps and surveillance on some of these guys?"

"What do you have? And it better be good."

"Found a cufflink tied to Carpozzi in a car used in the hit-and-run."

"I thought the car was still missing. How do you know that's his cufflink?"

"The car is still gone, but we're working on it. I got an informant about the cufflink."

"Jack, bring me some real evidence, then we'll talk about going to a judge to get some wiretaps."

"Keep pressing. I know you want these guys, but don't rush it."

"But chief, I need to get in on the inside to see what's going on."

"I'm on my way back to Washington tonight. I'll see what additional help I can get you. That's all for now."

Chapter Forty-Three

"Hey, guys, what's on the schedule today?" Dex was seated at the breakfast table munching on a cinnamon bun and hoping the kids would watch the Eagles football game on TV with him. More to get some bonding time with the kids than watch a potential losing season getting worse.

"I'd love to, Dad, but I'm going over to Bill's house with a bunch of the kids from the crew team, but we can catch up later," Jamie said as he gulped down his cereal and was off.

"Gee, Dad, I thought you were going out like you always do, so I made plans to see my friends, but maybe later today we can throw a football around like we used to," said Brett. Dex took a long sip of coffee, sighed, and watched as the table emptied.

Even Pojo got up and walked to another part of the house. "Great, even the dog doesn't know me anymore."

Donna who was in the kitchen getting a second cup of coffee returned to her seat and looked at her husband. "The boys are growing up and starting to have their own lives. It's nice and sad both at the same time."

"Do you think I'm a good father?"

Donna knew this was not a good time to lecture her husband and he was really a great father. "Sure, dear."

"I don't seem to spend much time with them lately, and one day they'll be grown and I won't even recognize them. I feel like that song *Cat in the Cradle*. The guy grew up before he even knew his sons."

"I love you, but even we don't ever seem to have much time together like we used to. Dex, you're overworked, and with all that's happening, you just need to relax, and maybe we should get away for a few days."

"I feel so damn guilty about what happened to Trolly. Why didn't I just tell him to stay home that night? When I see him in the hospital with all those tubes, I want to scream."

"It's not your fault. Stop beating yourself up. Try to help him instead of blaming yourself."

"Val is no better and she's a mess. How could it go so wrong?"

"Dear—"

"All they really wanted was to sing and write beautiful music together."

"You can't change the world. There is good and there is bad and evil. Sometimes life is unfair, but we have so much to be thankful for—our love, two great kids, and you really like what you do."

"Sometimes I just want to chuck it all in and do something else, maybe even teach full time or get a job in a company and not have so many people depend on me to make the right decisions for them."

"Is this a one or four o'clock game?" This was a signal from Donna the conversation was over. "I think I'll go to the store first and come back in time to see the game with you."

"It's at one. Maybe I'll run over to the hospital and visit Trolly and watch the first half with him, okay?"

Donna got up and touched her husband's arm, and he smiled.

"Dex, good to see you, man. I thought I'd have to watch the Eagles alone, and the way they been playing lately..."

"Glad to see you're feeling better. You always complain about them."

"Man, we've got to talk. I heard a lot of things from Val that I'm not proud of, but she wanted to level with me if we were to have a chance to really make it and I was too embarrassed to tell you. I didn't think you needed to know, but we have no secrets between us but now they might be important so here goes."

"Slow down a minute. When did you hear this stuff?"

"The first time was several months ago when we started getting together and Val one night told me about that boxer you represent Don, whatever his name was, and how he was set up by Carpozzi to lose. Val did some things I'd rather not discuss. Her payoff was to get the record contract, and she wanted fame so bad...you know how it is."

"Yes, I did hear something about that situation but not all the details."

"There's more, much more, like that football player was also set up to throw a game and blackmailed but something went wrong, and it gets really bad—"

"What player? What are you talking about?"

"You know the guy you were in Vegas with, that quarterback, and all the trouble he got in? Dex, Val did some things, and I'm scared for her. She knows too much, and

Sammy tried to shut her up. Carpozzi can't let her talk. I think I was a warning to her to shut up."

"Why did you keep all this a secret?"

"I love her, man, and I didn't want you lecturing me about how bad she was for me, and you know you would."

Dex started to protest, but Trolly cut him off.

"There's more about Carpozzi she knows, and he won't stop until she's quieted for good. Also, word on the street is the football kid you liked and tried to help was tied to that agent who's tied to Carpozzi and his buddies, and they beat up another agent really bad when he tried to sign the kid. The kid had no choice."

Dex's thoughts were churning when Trolly looked at him. "So what do I say to that cop who wants to talk to me?"

"There's more?"

"What about Val, what does she do or say?"

Dex sat still and thought back to the phone call with his buddy Jerry. The dean was right. He was over his head with this kind of criminal law advice, and he said, "Hold tight and don't say anything until I get back to you."

He got up to leave and Trolly blurted, "What about the Eagles game?"

"Screw it. They'll win or lose or tie." Trolly laughed at his friend's sudden indifference to football.

Dex thought about stopping in to visit Val but quickly changed his mind and headed home. He turned on the radio to 94.1 WYSP and heard the deep voice of Merrill Reese, the play-by-play announcer, just describing an Eagles touchdown. If the Eagles could win when they were behind, maybe there was a way to get everybody out of this mess.

Chapter Forty-Four

Monday morning, the weather was bleak, and the grayness outside matched his mood. Dex took a quick shower, dressed, ate breakfast almost in total silence, and kissed Donna as he hurried out the door.

He decided to call Conners and tell him to set up interviews with Val and Trolly. In exchange for them telling all he'd get immunity for the pair. No, he would tell Val and Trolly to say and admit nothing. It was the job of the police to find the criminals, and they had to play it in silence. Dex thought about everything and finally admitted to himself he didn't know what to do. Some super smart attorney he was, he just plain didn't know what was best for his clients and even more, his friends. What would you do if you were facing this choice? Dex asked over and over. He decided when he got to the office to call a few of the better known criminal defense attorneys and check that they had no conflicts in representing Val and Trolly. Actually, there might be a conflict in representing the two as they might have different defenses. It was time to bring some big guns into the case.

Dex, for a fleeting second, also wondered if he needed to be represented by counsel.

"Prof, glad to see you. There's a producer from *60 Minutes* on the phone, and he wants to speak with you," Sara said the minute he entered his office.

"Don't you ever go to class anymore? What are you doing here?"

"I knew you needed me. So you taking the call or what?"

"Yes, ring it in." He headed to his office and picked up the phone. "Good morning. What can I do for you?"

"We want the first exclusive interview with your clients and you can also be on the air with them in case of pending legal actions."

"I don't know if we're doing any interviews period. Let me get back to you."

"Well we're running a story, and we thought you might want to respond and at least get a chance to tell your side."

"What are you talking about?"

"You know about Val and her role in the Darrell Scott football attempted blackmail and extortion plot."

"What the hell are you talking about?"

"Well we thought you would know. You were in Vegas with them at the time it took place, right?"

Dex felt the wind sucking out of his chest and immediately got that sick feeling in his stomach. This mess was ever expanding and growing out of control and too fast to be defensive. He had to act and get back on the offense.

"Give me a day to speak to my clients. They're still in the hospital, so I'll get back to you."

"We hear the hospital is releasing Val today so please give us a call. Also, it would greatly help if you had a few pictures, bio, and a couple copies of her CD sent to me."

"Let me check what I have."

"I already gave your assistant my address."

Dex hung up and headed out to the reception area. "Sara, find the last package you got from Val and get out her pictures, bio, and CDs and get them ready to send to New York. I'm on my way to the hospital to see Val. I'll be back in a couple of hours."

When Dex arrived at Val's room, she was almost back to her pretty self, wearing street clothes and makeup and awaiting her discharge papers.

"Hi. I didn't know you were getting out."

"The doctor told me if I take it easy, I could go home."

Not waiting for more of an explanation, Dex told Val, "We need to talk and we need it right now. You better tell me the truth and start from the beginning."

"I was born in a small town down south—"

"Cut it out, Val. What the hell is with you, and what's going on?"

Tears welled up in her eyes and she started to tell Dex everything right down to the camera hidden in a teddy bear and what they did to Darrell Scott to her tryst with Dex's boxer friend and her role in his loss.

"Sammy's cousin was working on the football player, and when it went all wrong, the cousin disappeared." She spoke excitedly and jumped around but the pieces were starting to make a real ugly picture.

Two of Val's friends were taking her home and staying the night with her so Dex told her to tell no one anything and he would call her to see how she was.

As he sped back to the office, almost by habit, he called Sara. "What's new? Any calls?"

"Nothing important but when I opened the package of Val's and dumped it on the desk, you're never gonna believe what came out."

"Sara, don't make me guess. Just tell me."

"Okay, but you won't believe it. Beside the CDs there is a teddy bear and it's not even new. There is something inside it, honest."

"Don't move. Don't even breathe a word to anyone. Hold on to that teddy and don't tell a single person."

"Okay but—"

"No buts. Just hold on. I'll be there in 20 minutes."

Fifteen minutes later, Dex parked and literally ran to his office building.

The teddy was kind of worn and Dex immediately saw there were holes for the eye slots, and he felt something round in the teddy's rump, he located a zipper, which he unzipped and out rolled a disc.

"Well what have we here looks like it's a disc run from a computer," exclaimed Dex.

"Can I see it?"

"Better you don't."

"It's only fair. I found it."

Dex and Sara walked back to the library and inserted the disc, which contained page after page of record company business lists, payoffs and lists of gamblers who took part in the action on a particular Monday Night Football game.

"Holy mother, what have we here?"

Dex quickly understood this disc had enough data to put Carpozzi away for years.

Connecting the dots as any police forensic investigator would likely do would result in indictments sufficient to bring down many connected individuals.

Chapter Forty-Five

Jack Conners was no fool. A former marine officer who had seen combat action in Nam, he had a master's degree in criminal justice and soon after joining the force, he was quickly advancing with several valor citations for acts of bravery. Yet he knew the futility of red tape and jumping the chain of command.

His immediate chief had said no warrants or wire taps without more evidence, and that was the way it would be until something was uncovered. His years of experience told him he was closing in on Carpozzi, and he just needed the right key to unlock the door.

Connor's upbringing and perseverance were what parents dream about—Eagle Scout, varsity football team captain in high school, and good grades in college. A breakup with his college sweetheart became one of the turning points that changed the direction of his life. Still smarting from the disillusion of love lost, he joined the marines, and after basic training, he was chosen to go to officer training school.

Served with valor and wounded in action, after his discharge, he had decided to join the force.

Having fought for his country and close to losing his life from wounds fighting the bad guys, he had decided to dedicate his being to protecting the citizens from criminals.

He despised the Carpozzi type of guy who by force and intimidation were takers and never contributed to the good of society.

He was staring at the chart mounted on his wall, waiting as if by magic for an answer that would appear when his phone rang.

"Conners is here."

"Jack, this is Dex. I want to meet with you, and bring that FBI buddy of yours and also someone I can trust from the DA."

"What's up? I'm glad you called. I want to speak to Trolly and Val anyway."

"I might—and underscore the word *might*—have something that would be of interest to you and the investigation, but if you find something of real value, I need to be assured Trolly and Val are okay."

"What do you have that would be of such interest? It would have to be really something to cut a deal, and if everyone is so innocent, why would they need a deal?"

"I'll call you by tomorrow to set up a meeting."

"Why not today?"

Dex ignored his question. "Val is leaving the hospital, do you think you could get a squad car to watch her place?"

"Man, you better come clean. Talk to me."

"Can't. Just call it attorney-client confidentiality for now. Take care of your arrangements, and I'll call tomorrow."

Conners put the phone down, pulled out his card index, and placed a call to the district attorney. Next, he placed another call.

Think, man, think. Dex mulled over the call he had just placed and decided to get some help. He knew a number of really smart Philadelphia criminal defense lawyers and they don't use the term 'Philadelphia Lawyer' for just any reason. The term was coined centuries before when Andrew Hamilton, a Philadelphia lawyer, was called upon to defend a New York case which no one else wanted, and ever since, Philadelphia has had a reputation for having tough and smart lawyers. Dex looked through his list but each time he started to call, he feared a possible conflict, and he felt uneasy even alerting them to what he had, when it hit him. Of course, there was somebody he trusted who had been a criminal lawyer in his prior life.

He picked up the phone. "Dean, I really need a big favor."

"Yo, Dex, what's up, I have a faculty meeting in a couple of minutes so I'll get back to you."

"No, Jer, I need a really big favor, and you've got to help. Let me fill you in, so don't jump off."

Several minutes later after Jerry had heard all of the last few days' events he told Dex, "I haven't practiced law in several years. Besides, I'm a dean and can't get involved, but what you're talking about is requesting complete immunity. Also, you want some kind of witness protection and new identities, and you need the approval of several layers of DA and the feds as well, and it must be in writing."

"See, you know exactly what to do. Please, I'm begging, and I'll spring for dinner and tickets to the Eagles game. Take a couple days off. You haven't seen the kids in a while. Bring your wife. I really appreciate this and you're saving my neck."

"Buddy, I'd like to help, but—"

"Besides, don't you teach your students about justice and the American way, and now you get a chance to show them by your example."

"Stop already. Yeah, it's like law school all over again. I'll call you back when I check arrival times."

Dex thought, *Okay take a deep breath and relax, breath in deeply, exhale, and close your eyes.* "Damn. All those years of martial arts training, and nothing is working," he muttered.

He put on his suit jacket, walked over to one of his favorite joints, and ordered a single shot of scotch.

"You alright? Never saw you take a drink except for an occasional beer," said the bartender.

"Lot on my mind."

It worked a lot faster than breathing exercises. Taking a sip, he leaned back and smiled. He knew he had made the right choice.

He would still have to fill Trolly and Val in on what he planned, and no better time than the moment.

Trolly was getting better day by day, but was still bothered by a ringing in his ears which the doctors still believed would dissipate.

He trusted Dex completely but couldn't understand the need for any of this lawyering stuff. He felt he was a victim and had done nothing wrong. Still, if his trusted friend and lawyer thought this was best for him and Val, he was okay with the concept. He wanted to get Carpozzi at all costs, and if this was the way to go he decided they'd do it and get that son of a bitch.

"Good. Let's talk to Val and explain my plan."

"Wait a sec. Did you say I got to relocate?"

"Well, it makes sense so we avoid any problems."

"No place real hot, and they better like my music."

"Who doesn't like your music anywhere?"

Dex looked at his friend and thought, *This is not as easy as I hoped it would be,* but decided to say no more for the time being.

Val was an easy sell on the idea. In fact, she loved the thought of escaping with Trolly and starting all over, anywhere just so the Vince Carpozzis of the world would leave her and Trolly alone. She startled Dex by asking, "Will you still be allowed to be my lawyer when I get my career going again?"

He smiled but didn't answer.

Chapter Forty-Six

Jerry's plane was late for takeoff and about 45 minutes late in arriving, so while Dex sat and waited, he thought about his friend.

They had met the first week of law school and immediately became fast friends. Jerry was slightly heavy, not athletic, but had that quick sense of humor that made him popular in a crowd. In class, he always knew the answer but didn't volunteer. He was laid back and didn't speak just to hear himself. It seems those who ask a thousand questions in class and always are ready to argue a point end up the C students. Those who are quiet and listen are the ones who, when the grades come out, surprise the class at how high they place. Jerry was second in the class the first year and first both second and third year and had the pick of large firms to join. The friendship went beyond studying together, and by the third year, they realized they would be close for life. Often the two and their wives would go out together, if just for pizza and beers; they shared the same hopes and desires for each other.

Dex and he talked about starting their own firm one day, but both understood it was more desire and talk than reality. Jerry was big firm and big starting salary immediately.

Play the game and one day you are the partner, the one with four windows in your office. Dex leaned back in his car and smiled. How sad you measure your life by the number of windows in your office. One or two, associate level, three junior partner, four windows, full partner and if you got to five or a corner office, they were reserved for managing partner or maybe executive committee. The guys who set the salary and bonus for the members of the firm. Placed in the litigation section, the partners soon realized Jerry's exceptional ability and he was involved in complex litigation including white-collar criminal defense and Racketeering Influenced Corrupt Organizations Act (RICO) actions, which dealt with criminal enterprise and racketeering.

After one long and complex case in which Jerry successfully defended and got an acquittal for a firm client he despised and believed was guilty, he abruptly left the firm and accepted a teaching position at the law school where after a number of years he was now dean.

As the plane landed and passengers deplaned, Dex spotted his friend. He was gray at the temples, slightly heavier, and wore those wireless rimmed eyeglasses that scream professor or academic.

"Hey, bud. How was the flight? Write any law review articles instead of watching the in-flight movie?"

He nodded, reached out to Dex, and they hugged.

Jerry came without his wife and explained he was staying only for a day or so until the immunity plea agreement with Trolly and Val was settled and he needed to do some more research on WestLaw, a computerized research engine about indemnity law. Dex smiled. He couldn't remember the last time he used WestLaw in his entertainment practice, although his associate and Sara did on occasion.

"Fine. Let's go back to my office, go out to dinner, discuss the case, and catch up."

"Sounds like a plan."

"Better call Donna and tell her we're not coming home for dinner. I see so little of her and the kids lately. There has to be a better way."

His friend heard the remark but didn't answer.

As they entered the Palm restaurant, two former classmates happened to come in, so the four had a drink at the bar and caught up on all the years that had passed so quickly, joking and reminiscing about past exams and professors.

At dinner seated in a booth away from the crowd, the two men held a much more serious conversation.

Jerry quizzed Dex as if he were preparing for trial and kept returning to the computer disc and its contents. Jerry had already made Dex burn several copies and the original was to be placed in a safe deposit box for safekeeping.

Jerry was excited, and Dex sensed his friend missed preparing and working on cases. He could tell Jerry was actually enjoying the crisis, and Dex wondered if he would like teaching full time and being away from all this tumult. *Is no one ever totally satisfied with their life, and is the grass actually ever greener?* Dex thought but did not speak for this was not the night for philosophical discussion.

By the next afternoon Jerry had nailed down his research and was speaking, but almost lecturing to Dex and Sara, who was absolutely enthralled with the dean and his manner.

Jerry also wanted someone at the meeting who could be trusted from the U.S. attorney's office and the state attorney general's office as well.

A call to Conners was not well received. "Are you nuts? I already am out on a limb with the people coming and I'll get chopped if this isn't worthwhile."

"Trust me it is, and I have a stake in this as well. Remember, these two mean a lot to me."

"Don't play me, but I'll see what I can do."

"Jack, we need to meet in a secret place, and you've got to trust the people you bring. I'm relying on you."

"How about the White House and CIA?" he replied sarcastically.

"Not a bad idea...Only kidding, but you'll be more than satisfied."

"I'll be back to you, but why the state attorney general?"

Dex replied, "Remember Elliot Spitzer, the New York attorney general? He chased and subpoenaed several big record companies—Sony, EMI, UMG, and others—and got I think, settlements with several for alleged pay-for-play. He's now after radio companies. Too bad he's running for governor. He really has them scared."

Conners was now paying careful attention and began to understand where Dex was headed. "I'll be back to you. Do you want company?"

"What do you mean?"

"Police protection."

"Hell no. I don't want any attention," Dex said, beginning to realize his life was changing. "Do you think I need it?"

"Talk to you tomorrow, and take care of yourself."

Turning to Jerry, Dex said, "Can you imagine me an entertainment lawyer, and now I'm in a scene from a crime movie."

"You. What about me, a dean of a law school? What the hell am I doing here?"

"I think you're loving it," Dex said as both men high-fived.

"Tain le hamesh."

"What's that mean?"

Jerry answered, "Gimme five, in Hebrew."

Chapter Forty-Seven

The following morning, a brief telephone call established a meeting at three in the afternoon at an address in a small, nondescript building about an hour or so driving time located outside of Philadelphia.

Jerry and Dex attended without clients and were escorted into a conference room with Jack Conners, his immediate superior local police detective, two special agents of the FBI, both wearing pilot-type sunglasses, an assistant DA, two representatives of the state attorney general's office, two DEA agents, and a couple of women who remained nameless, one from the justice department, the other from some kind of agency Dex didn't quite catch. He thought he heard something like Homeland Security Agency but that would really be a reach. Nobody really made an effort to identify them.

There was also a guy who looked like a middle-aged accountant with about four pencils and pens stuffed into a plastic pocket protector in his breast pocket.

"Gentlemen, ladies, nice to meet you. I'm Dex Randle, an attorney for Val Clifton and Will 'Trolly' Turner, both of whom have been the victims of brutal attacks."

Several attendees nodded. "With me is Dean Jerry Hall, a former law classmate who is assisting me with our clients."

The people at the table once again nodded.

Conners spoke, "Dex, you told me you had some valuable information that could assist us in this ongoing investigation, so what do you have?"

"Well, let's say I might have some information in disc form showing certain corrupt activities of certain individuals that would be of keen interest to you, and further, it's also possible we could provide firsthand testimony of some shocking actions that are criminal in nature. Of course, we are concerned about the protection of our clients from any further harm."

"Mr. Randle, no offense is meant, but you are sounding like a bad movie production. What do you have, and what do you want?" the lady from the Justice Department spoke as the others held back laughter.

"This might be a joke to you but to my clients it's life and death—serious business."

Conners jumped in, "Dex, of course it is, but we need to know what this is all about."

Dex looked at Conners for a moment, then at Jerry who nodded, as Dex took a copy of the disc and put it on a laptop for all to see. "Okay as you can see, it's page upon page of payouts to promotion men and radio program directors to buy their way onto the station play lists, violating federal law. The next pages show interstate illegal gambling, betting, blackmail, extortion, and more, all used to fix an NFL game."

"Where did you get this?" The assembled group was now paying rapt attention to Dex.

Ignoring the question, Dex continued, "We are also prepared to get firsthand evidence and testimony as to intimidation, professional boxing fixes, filing false tax returns,

248

attempted murder, and illegal drug trafficking. I hope that is very clear." He used his best stare-down technique toward the lady from the Justice Department.

This time she quietly said, "Yes."

"If you are interested in going any further at this time, Dean Hall will discuss what we want and expect for our clients' cooperation and testimony. Do I make myself very clear?" Dex sat down, and there was silence.

Now, that's the Dex I know and love, thought Jerry, but he held back a smile. "Well that's a mouthful to digest. Would you and the dean allow us a few minutes of privacy to discuss this before we continue?" one of the sunglass-wearing FBI agents asked.

Dex and Jerry stood, and Dex reached over, closed the laptop, and took it with him.

As they closed the door behind them, the group took a collective breath and finally one said, "Wow, where do we begin?"

"These guys are no fools and this is the kind of break we have been waiting for months to get," said one of the agents.

"There is enough info in that disc to find everything we need," said the guy with the pocket protector. "How do you think they got it?"

"Listen, we were never after these two anyway, I was trying to throw a scare into them to get what they know," spoke up Jack.

The detective said, "Yeah, but Val was part of some of this stuff and…"

The detective was abruptly cut off by the assistant DA, "You want the minnow or the sharks who can lead us to the whales?"

At this point, almost by instinct, they all looked at the two women, the first from the Justice Department, who felt rather foolish after her initial comment to Dex. "I'm all for it."

The second lady, somewhat older but clearly the kind that commanded attention and respect when she spoke, cleared her throat, "Homeland Security is interested, along with the DEA, in tracking the source of the drugs that are coming in and the money trail to see if it helps enemies of our nation."

She continued, "FBI have been instructed to follow our lead, and so the chain of command is you all will report to me, but I emphasize this, there is enough for everybody to get their credit. I do not expect confusion or bickering over who runs what.

"For the time being, state and local will appear to head the case. For reasons best unsaid, Jack is the liaison and no one is assigned to this task force without my permission. Don't discuss this case unless there is an absolute need to know with anyone, and make sure you trust them.

"Speaking of trust, each of you has been hand-picked, there is no accident that each of you is in this room today and you all have important roles to fulfill. I can tell you without disclosing more that your government on high thanks you for providing this service to your country.

"Are there any questions?"

"Where are we working from and how do we handle our regular assignments?" asked the Assistant State Attorney General.

"Each of you have been cleared to work from here and you don't need your bosses' approval, it's already been cleared and they think this is a cooperative local and state combined task force and 'sting operation' to catch some bad guys."

"Well it is, isn't it?" said the ASAG.

The lady from the Justice Department spoke, "Now let's meet those two and present our limited indemnity proposal and not a word about what this is really about. The limited indemnity will keep them cooperative and under our control.

"Basically, we sweat them and then give in to whatever they want. I got the feeling they are already prepared so make it appear we got to get approval from our bosses."

"Gentlemen, thank you for presenting this evidence today," intoned the assistant DA upon their return. "We have all agreed to grant your request, and in anticipation of that request, I have prepared this written agreement for your review." Jerry and Dex were handed two copies. "I know you will need some time to review the document and you can do so now or if you prefer take it with you, we can meet tomorrow."

Jerry scanned the document and looked up. "Let's not play games. This is only a conditional and at best limited indemnity. We all know how important this is or you all would not be sitting here and no way does DEA, FBI, AG, and the rest of heaven knows alphabet agencies sit together unless all hell is breaking loose, and bluntly that is not our concern. Let me finish," he said, when the justice department lady started to speak.

251

"Here is a document we prepared." He handed out ten copies to the assembled group, which immediately let them know Jerry and Dex had anticipated and assumed such a gathering.

"Please note our agreement calls for full immunity at the local, state, and federal level, and oh yes, we need to decide where our clients are to be located and protected."

Dex jumped in, "Not only relocated but with new identities, and records to back up their new identities."

Jerry then picked up on Dex's theme. "Further, there is a reasonable list of items they will need to assist them in relocating and putting their new lives together."

The two women looked at each other but did not utter a sound.

"They are not criminals and you are asking a great deal from both of them. Of course, they will cooperate fully and give you whatever information they possess. I would respectfully hope you can review this document, get your bosses' approval, which I'm sure you already have, and when we get the signed documents, we'll turn over all we have and make Mr. Turner and Ms. Clifton available. Thank you for your time."

Jerry and Dex got up, and without another word walked out of the conference room. The assembled group sat in silence.

"Glad they are not trying the case," said the assistant DA, and got some glaring looks.

In the car, Dex looked at his friend. "Dean Hall, you're the best."

Jerry smiled back. "You're right up there as well."

252

Dex replied, "Randle and Hall, attorneys at law. What a dream team."

"How about dean and full-time professor," Jerry countered.

Both men sat in silence and thought whatever men think about when all is not well. If there is a time in one's life when he is content, neither man for his own separate reasons, had yet arrived at that time.

Chapter Forty-Eight

The next morning, Dex and Jerry were sitting in Dex's law office drinking coffee and Jerry eating donuts while Dex refused his offer to touch one of them, when the phone call came from Conners. "The powers that be have accepted your terms and are signing off on the documents, so we would like to meet with your clients and ask some questions and get statements and the original disc. We, of course, will want to know how the disc came into your possession, how to verify its authenticity, and of course who got it."

"I'll arrange a time for you to speak with them. Do you think they need protection now, or is it still safe since no one knows what's taking place?"

"I think the less attention drawn to them, the better for now. Dex, I never said this, but real nice work by you and the dean yesterday. They were caught short by the presentation."

"Thanks for your help."

"Jer, they agreed to our terms, so we've got to get moving."

"Just slow up a minute. I agreed to help you out on the indemnity agreement meeting. I have to really get back to my law school."

Dex had chosen to forget he and Jerry were not partners, and he looked at Jerry as if to say stay and be a part of this.

"You're right. I do love working with you but I'm going back, and maybe when this mess is all over you will want to join me in teaching," said Jerry.

The two men hugged as Jerry wheeled his bag down the hall and both men again stood in silence awaiting the elevator.

From the time of the previous day's meeting, the task force of government officials had been electrified by first, the disc and its information, but also the prospect of firsthand and eyewitness accounts of some of the dealing, and it really pushed them into action. Much documentation was being prepared to take to a federal judge who could authorize not only phone wiretaps, but e-mail taps as well. When the right time was determined, bank records would also be subpoenaed. Surveillance schedules were being drawn up, and the task force was bringing in additional people to conduct investigations and interviews.

There is a constant struggle between the desire to garner information and yet, at the same time, protect the rights of the individual. As new technology gets developed, it often outpaces the laws protecting the individual and the government has not only much new sophisticated technology, but with the RICO Act and the Patriot Act, more room to maneuver. The right channels need to be legally addressed and followed not so much because of the desire to be diligent in applying the law, but to make sure good evidence does not get thrown out because of how it was acquired. The evidence must not become tainted. If somehow they could get close to the computers, with the electronic devices at their disposal, they could literally break passwords and record computer messages being sent and received. They ruled out trying to get into Carpozzi's home, but the record company could be approached by a team acting as a late night cleaning crew that could plant some listening devices and quickly leave the premises.

The first meeting, after Dex had received the signed copies of his agreements, was scheduled with Val, who had been prepped and rehearsed. As much as he prepared Val, nothing could prime her for questions coming from every angle, being asked by prosecutors with years of trial and questioning experience. The first story about Don 'the Bomber' Carson and his torrid night with Val, while intriguing, was not what the group was after. Several members of the task force were interested in finding the video but Dex thought it was more to see the action than for legal reasons. More interest was shown with the gambling, blackmail, and extortion plot with Darrell Scott, the quarterback.

Agents would be visiting Q's wife and getting copies of the tape.

The federal agents were very interested in the supplying of drugs, who was doing the supplying, how the money was transferred to the supplier, and if any of the money was going to countries with agendas against the United States. Val though questioned about the attack on her, was really interrogated about the quantity of drugs that Sammy had on his person. Where did he get it? What had she personally witnessed? Was she aware of any suppliers? Was she a user?

The state's attorney general and justice were very interested in the record company documents showing pay-for-play and violations of several acts. A team of agents pressured record promoters and radio executives to give up Carpozzi and his operation.

The local police were gearing toward the tie-in of Sammy to Carpozzi and his assault, the hit-and-run on Trolly and tying the disappearance and murder of Carpozzi's associates.

Val even talked about the tie-in of the young football player's agent and how she overheard talk about the severe beating of a competitor agent who tried to represent Trent Prichard, tying this to Carpozzi's cronies. Dex, just to be sure, reread the indemnity agreement after that session.

By the time Val told them what she knew, many yellow tablets of notes were quickly filling the files, and this was but the first of many such sessions to come.

Trolly, by contrast, while still in the hospital, was interviewed by Conners and another federal agent who seemed to push in the direction of the ongoing feud and jealousy of Carpozzi.

"Did Trolly have any other enemies who would do this?"

"Had there been any threats to Trolly by Carpozzi or his associates?"

"Did Carpozzi owe him royalties?"

"What was he doing at such a late hour going out?"

"Why so many donuts?" This question had even Dex perplexed.

Dex for his part was now spending a portion of each day involved in sessions with Val and Trolly. He needed to keep his everyday life in order, maintaining the rest of his active practice, teaching, and still have time for Donna and the kids. He desired to maintain a normal front and didn't even discuss the details of the questioning with Donna, who seemed to instinctively understand to let him be.

Dex was under the constant pressure of balancing the two inconsistent points: appear normal and not bring attention to Val, Trolly, or himself. He was still trying to figure out when the right time was to insist they go into protective custody and then federal witness protection.

For the next several weeks, Dex was calling Jerry almost daily, giving reports and getting opinions and advice. The bond was once again growing between them. Jerry, offered strategy, then listened to Dex give his thinking and then the two formulated their collective strategy.

"Dex, you're right. I'm getting to anticipate your calls and enjoy our give and take."

"It's got to beat marking exams for the rest of your life. Damn, I really didn't mean what I just said." Dex attempted to apologize but deep within, he was glad he said it. Perhaps it would make Jerry change his mind. Dex loved the sound of Randle and Hall, attorneys at law, as it rolled off his tongue.

Chapter Forty-Nine

"Dear, what will we do, and how are we going to earn a living if we move away?" Val had a stream of questions and though Trolly kept reassuring her, he himself had many questions and doubts.

Where will we be located? he thought. *Won't Val be recognized?* "We'll be together at last, and we have our love and our music," he said.

"What music? If we're hidden, how can we get our music out?"

"I'll call Dex and we can set up a meeting and get some answers."

The feds had established timelines with respect to investigations and interviews of witnesses with a determination to present all the evidence to a grand jury and get an indictment. Meanwhile, there was much to do once the wiretaps were in place. Forensic accountants were in place to trace the financial records, bank statements and track and follow the flow of the money. Especially, they were interested in the flow of the drugs and payments—how the deals were made, where the drugs originated, coordinating any foreign agencies, and how the drugs were distributed.

A second group concentrated on the disc record reports— who got payoffs, how they were made, whether songs get special treatment, and whether they played on the radio as a result of the payments.

Investigators were spreading across the country and questioning radio program directors and DJs. Each interviewer used the scare technique, cautioning them to not breathe a word to anyone about these interviews and making each individual feel as if he or she alone were the target of the investigation. Quickly in exchange for their not being charged, they were only too happy to tell all they knew and, in a number of cases, gave up the promotion people who had made 'contributions' to them for getting airplay or at the least provided valuable leads or information.

Even more agents and computer geeks were assigned to examine the gambling lists. Certain bookies in exchange for being left alone turned over much info about the betting taking place for that one certain NFL game and the betting patterns. Two agents visited Q's home, and his ex-wife reluctantly turned over the videotape of the night in Vegas. Q, with his attorney present, also was quizzed about the situation and the conversations with the mystery voice, and the threats were somehow located and reconstructed by painstaking efforts of FBI field agents.

The dark green SUV was traced back to its original lease from an auto dealership in New Jersey. What interested the investigators was the unusual payout of the lease but not the return of the car to the dealership where it was originally purchased. Backtracking, local police traced leads to the car compactor, and one of the men working that night gave a statement of how a green SUV was brought in and who he saw that evening.

The cufflink match was finally made to a store in a casino in Vegas where Carpozzi had made the purchase of a similar pair.

Many people criticize the bigness of government but those who go up against the government, or have them investigating, especially when all three levels, local, state and federal are working together, are usually no match for the money, talent and time they are willing to expend to get their man.

Bigness begets bigness and with any organization of many individuals and competing egos, there was some clashing of territorial jurisdiction. Not to be overlooked were the political overtones surrounding the entire procedure. Though downplayed initially, each agency had its own agenda and the levels of government, though all wanting the same result were cautious of who would get the credit and who would make what announcement. It was decided the agencies involved could take no further chances of one agency trying to gain some notoriety or someone prematurely letting some word escape and blowing several months of preparation. At a meeting of the task force, it was decided to press for a grand jury to hear the evidence and once they had the charges and indictment returned, to schedule simultaneous raids and arrests on Carpozzi, his associates, several drug dealers, and a few representative pay-for-play recipients, including the vice president of the large network, Mr. Peters. A picture of the visibly shaken executive handcuffed and being lead to a waiting police car shook all the others who had taken payments, and they would all sing in return for special treatment. They would fall over themselves to cut deals in return for their testimony and escape prosecution and embarrassment.

"I want two detectives stationed with Val and Trolly, and we need to get their paperwork processed because the heat will be coming any day," Conners said.

One of the FBI agents said, "Four of my boys on a rotating basis will also be used to join in the protection detail."

"I'm going to call Dex and inform him so he gets them ready." Conners looked at the assembled group. "We as a unit have worked hard for this, and it's not over. The hard part is still to come." Smiling, he added, "I don't know about any of you, but I got dibs on a really early raid and arrest on that bastard Carpozzi. I want to personally wake him up."

Dex sat with Val and Trolly. "This is not easy but during the course of the ongoing investigation and subsequent trial, the two of you will be kept together in an undisclosed location with personal police protection, and when this mess is all over, you will be moved to an undisclosed location and set up with new identities and a stake in forging a new life, but the old stuff and ways are left behind."

"But, what about you for instance, how do we stay in touch?"

"Yes, what do we do about my singing career?"

"The important thing is to keep both of you safe and together," Dex said.

"When does all this take place? How much advance notice?" Val softly asked.

"You're getting it now, and tonight it starts."

Dex wasn't quite sure how all this played out, but he didn't want to alarm his friends. He wasn't sure if even he would know the location. Perhaps, it would be best not to know the exact location.

Chapter Fifty

The task force was moving forward, pressing to get sufficient evidence to take the case to the grand jury. Conners, with the help of the DA and the state attorney's office, had persuaded the federal judge to order and approve wiretaps both of the phone lines as well as e-mails. Surveillance was now being carried out in shifts. Carpozzi's home, record company, even his hangouts were closely watched.

Carpozzi and his very astute team of criminal defense lawyers, though not aware of the taps and specifics of what was transpiring, were very aware of potential trouble coming and were planning and taking all kinds of precautions to not expose themselves to anything that might aid the investigators.

At a closed and very private meeting and planning session, though the lawyers would not come out and tell their client directly to destroy evidence, they let it be known that harmful information on the computers would be best to be permanently deleted with no traces.

On the advice of their in-house lawyers, the running of the record company operations were now being conducted as a real record company with discussions of artist signings, on-air promotions, and meetings with artists and their management to plan careers and touring. It was the intention of the defense team to be able to show at the appropriate time this was a real company run and operated in a proper manner.

When the government is after an individual and believes there is sufficient evidence to contemplate an indictment or they are pursuing an individual, they usually will let that person know by means of a letter which in effect is a notice that the person is the target of the government.

No target letters had been issued by the government, and Carpozzi tried to be careful about his activities, but he was leading his life as he had done in the past, convinced no one would have the nerve to implicate him. Fear and intimidation had been his method of keeping everyone quiet in the past but now he dared not be out in the open.

Val and Trolly, who had been out of the limelight except for the recent publicity surrounding their attacks, were now in police protection and being quizzed daily about as much of the Carpozzi operation as they knew.

Pressure was coming down hard on the lesser players to spill what they knew, and many pieces of the puzzle were beginning to come together. The task force was going to be asking for charges against Carpozzi and his associates numbering at least a dozen or more, ranging from simple assault to attempted murder, income tax evasion, crossing state lines for extortion, blackmail, illegal gambling, pay-for-play as to illegal record promotion, and drug operations.

The task force had early on decided to let this case play out on the federal level rather than local courts, but certain carved-out areas would be reserved for local or state prosecutions as well. Adding another level of intensity in this case was trying to determine from where the drug supply was coming, and if any of the money trail would lead back to interests detrimental to the security of the nation. It was well known that certain groups of terrorists financed their operations by the sale of drugs. This led several departments of the federal government to lend their support to the investigation.

Conners, in his daily briefings with his team, was compiling more and more evidence of the enormity of the corruption. The forensic auditors were able to trace large sums of money being transferred from the record company to purchases of drugs. Payoffs to record promoters to give various and sundry illegal benefits were easily traced, and scared program directors were giving sworn statements when they or their attorneys realized the serious nature and how widespread the federal net was extending.

Q and his wife, who were making sincere efforts, even though divorced, to reconcile seemed to be drawn together when his wife realized how the football blackmail plot evolved. The local police and FBI were particularly interested in the person who was the contact on the phone calls and somehow were working on leads as to his disappearance and tying him and his death to the blackmail plot.

When several persons were brought in for questioning and faced with a long list of potential charges or telling what they knew, more than a few flipped and told their story. It was only a matter of time until word spread of the investigation. The task force was almost ready to go to the grand jury, and Carpozzi and some of the top associates were made aware they were targets of the investigation.

"Need to see you this afternoon at the zoo near the monkey cage." Carpozzi used his new cell phone and spoke quickly and quietly to someone on another cell phone. "See ya."

FBI, who had intercepted the call were in place dressed as maintenance men and zoo staff as they fanned out to await the meeting armed with intricate listening devices and even an expert lip reader.

"Can you get to that bitch and shut her up? She can't live to testify. Do whatever it takes. Fifty now and fifty more on finishing the job."

"Do you understand she's got two cops with her at all times?"

"So?"

"Two-fifty, and I don't know. Got to talk to some people. Word is they got all kinds of people involved in this case. I need to get back to you."

"Don't just get it done. We've got a deal. Two-fifty it is. If you get the dude, I'll throw in another hundred."

"Where is she?"

"My contact says she's still at her apartment, too dumb to even move her."

One of the FBI agents, on hearing the last comment was so incensed he had to be restrained from going after the two men and almost blew the cover. His partner said, "We got what we wanted and let's get back to the others and get this moving."

"How do they know where she is?"

"Don't know, but we better be careful. Somewhere there's a leak."

The assembled group, back in their offices was confident they had more than enough strong evidence backed by testimony to get an indictment.

"So, Ms. Prosecutor, we did our part, now show us what you can do."

"We'll be going to the grand jury shortly. Just protect the evidence and Val and Trolly."

Conners and two of the team he trusted had already moved Val and Trolly to a new and undisclosed location. He picked up the phone and heard Dex's voice. "Hi. No, nothing really new, but I'll keep you posted."

"Thanks, please keep in touch." Dex was somewhat annoyed by Conners' curt tone.

No one, unless they had a real need to know would be told anything. Too much was at stake.

Chapter Fifty-One

The decor of the grand jury room matched the sober testimony of the federal prosecutor as she presented the overwhelming evidence against Vince Carpozzi and several of his associates. The location was in the federal court building in downtown Philadelphia, and it conveyed the stark and oft times conservative nature of the city. This was serious business and was presented as such.

"Ladies and gentlemen of the grand jury..." On and on the testimony and records were introduced until it was evident that an indictment would be returned.

Conners and his task force, which had been augmented by many local and federal agents now armed with search and arrest warrants, would be conducting several and nearly simultaneous early-morning arrests in Philly and all across the country.

As the raids were being conducted and targets were arrested, they were read their Miranda rights—the right to remain silent, the right to an attorney, if you can't afford an attorney, one will be appointed...and the warning that anything said could be used against you.

The reading of these statements is a sobering realization that you are in deep trouble and your life as you then know it is changing in a way that affects your very being and all the people surrounding you. Your life will never again be the same. The mood at headquarters was jubilant. Conners and the task force were busy making preparations that had been anticipated and rehearsed a number of times.

"I'll lead the arrest at the Carpozzi residence. He's my special project, and I should only be so lucky to have him resist," Conners commented.

"How many vans are we taking?" said one agent as he buckled his bulletproof vest, then his blue windbreaker jacket with FBI stenciled across the back.

Teams of Philadelphia and New Jersey SWAT officers were also coordinated for the raid, and officers had been briefed to take positions blocking all entrances and exits. Though it was not believed they would be needed, battering rams to break down doors were also placed in the vehicles.

"I'd love to batter down his bedroom door with one of these babies." The officers looked at Conners and could see the excitement in his face.

Teams in New York, Atlanta, and Chicago were also preparing and being coordinated for their designated raids and arrests. The total concept was to affect an overall sweep and bring in as many as possible at the same time. This would have the added advantage of securing additional evidence before it could be destroyed. Shock and awe would have nothing on this team effort.

Two detectives and two additional federal agents were permanently assigned to protect Val and Trolly.

A knock on their door signaling they were to quickly dress and be ready to move again caused both to understand something was happening, but the four officers assigned to them said nothing other than they were being moved again for their protection.

"What do you think is happening?" Val whispered.

"I don't know, but something is up. We just got moved two days ago."

Val moved close to Trolly and gently hugged him, being careful not to touch his ribs. "I love you so much, but I'm scared."

"Shh shh, little darling, it will be alright, and when the trial is over, our lives will be perfect. Just you wait and see."

"Are we always going to be on the move?"

"No it will get better," he assured her.

"But how will we live and—"

Trolly interrupted, "Now is not the time. Hurry and get dressed. We're out of here."

"Let us lead and you follow, but stay close behind us." The officers escorted them out and into a van that pulled up as they emerged from the building.

Police cars and vans swarmed Carpozzi's residence, and the noise and hustle was designed to shock and awe those in the mansion.

"Jesus, there must be an army out there," said one of the bodyguards as he backed away from the window.

One look at the vast armada of heavily armed police convinced even the hardest and toughest of the people in the house that resistance would be futile. The teams took up their assigned positions and the planning they had practiced over and over now enhanced their movements.

True to his word, Conners, after quickly gaining entrance to the front, was one of the first to move up the hall steps, and with almost a simultaneous warning, threw open the bedroom door. It being only 6:00 A.M., Carpozzi was in his king-size bed almost sound asleep. When Conners read him his rights and reached across to cuff him, Carpozzi spat at him.

"You son of a bitch. Get out of here. I'll have my lawyers get me out in an hour."

Conners wiped his face and punched Carpozzi in the stomach causing him to double up and as he did, Conners hit him in the jaw and a tooth popped out in a spittle of blood.

One of the officers grabbed Conners and held him back, as some of the other officers intervened and got Carpozzi on his feet.

"Oh, that was a nasty fall Mr. Carpozzi. You really must be more careful when getting out of bed." Conners smiled while rubbing his fist. "Here let me help you up."

Several of the officers chimed in and added to the chorus as Conners started to look around the spacious room.

As officers streamed in and started boxing cartons of evidence, one officer examining a jewelry box whistled and exclaimed, "Lookie here. It looks like one diamond cufflink shaped like a dice. Wonder where the mate is?"

Computers were carried out along with packets of white powder. In the nightstand table next to the bed was a fully loaded automatic .45, and as the house was searched an arsenal of weapons was found.

"Don't hit your head on the door," Conners said as Carpozzi was roughly pushed into a police van.

Several of his associates were also rounded up and taken to the station.

"Call my lawyer, and tell him to meet me at the station," Carpozzi called out to one of the men standing next to the police car. Carpozzi turned to Conners. "This ain't over, and you're gonna pay."

Conners moved as if to hit him again and smiled. "You're right. It's not over. It's merely the beginning of the end for you."

Chapter Fifty-Two

Conners sat opposite Dex sipping coffee in the diner. "Well it's eight months later, and after all the legal maneuvering, it finally starts tomorrow. I want to thank you for your help and input."

Dex nodded as if to say he understood. The two genuinely had grown to be friends. "I just hope Val and Trolly can get on with their lives after they testify. Did you know she's pregnant and they are planning to get married?"

"No kidding? That's nice." Conners seemed sincere.

"I just hope Carpozzi gets all he deserves. You know he was in the car when they hit your friend."

"Why do you have such a personal hatred for this guy?"

"I don't actually. I just hate the way some guys think they are above the law and nothing applies to them, and he's evil."

"He probably has no conscience and no real feelings for anything," Dex said.

"He hurt so many people in this case and continues to flaunt the law, and somebody has to stop them, or there is no society and decent folk don't have a chance without us warriors to protect them."

"Didn't realize you were so profound."

"Bull, but don't play me. You're a warrior yourself. You've been doing it for years, protecting artists and athletes from superior business types who pretend to like them and at the same time take them for all they have."

"We don't admit or acknowledge it, but we're cut from the same tree."

"Thanks. I'd share a foxhole with you anytime. Enough of this hand holding, tomorrow it really counts. I just hope those smart-ass lawyers don't find some legal mumbo jumbo and get that guy off."

Dex smiled but didn't answer. He knew from experience with juries you just never know.

"See you tomorrow. I'll try and arrange for you to get some time alone with Trolly. He's been asking for you."

"Thanks. Breakfast is on me."

The last eight months or so had taken a toll on Dex, both over worry about Val and Trolly and in a deeper sense, he started having thoughts about life and its values.

Did he have the same love for his profession? Was there something else he could do that was more meaningful and helpful? He was restless, and not getting the same joy each day as he was used to, and the ugly side of all he had witnessed in the last year had made him question his values and what was really important. He paused for a moment, kind of hesitated, leaned forward, and in a low, cracking voice asked Sara to come in his office and close the door.

"Sara, you have a great future, and I'm really fond of you, and it's because of that and all that has transpired that I think you should take the other job offer from that large firm. It will be more than I would ever pay you, but to be honest, I've got to rethink my life and what I want to do."

Sara had tears in her eyes. "Prof, you could never stop practicing law. You love it, and I thought I'd work with you. I don't care about the money—really, I mean it."

"Let's table this until after the trial, but do not—I repeat do not—turn down this other job offer without first speaking to me."

Dex turned in that big lawyer chair and didn't really seem to care how big the chair was. That mentor who told him he could charge more if he had a big lawyer chair seemed light-years ago. Funny, but he didn't remember the mentor telling him about the big headaches that came along with the big chair.

He picked up the phone and dialed Donna. "Hi. Whatcha doing?"

"You alright? Your voice sounds…"

"I love you."

"I love you too. What's wrong? I hear that funny sound in your voice. How's your stomach feeling?"

"No, nothing is wrong. Maybe when this is all over we should go on a vacation and just get away."

"Now I know something's wrong. You hate vacations."

"I don't know. Gotta go. There's the other line. See you for dinner." He answered the other call.

"Mr. Randle, this is Evan Dougal, and I've been referred to you about my desire to put on a series of concerts. Part of the proceeds would go to a charity to help provide computers to schools unable to fund these purchases. My corporate attorney referred me to you, and I'd like to set up an appointment to come down and see you."

276

Dex thought, *I've really let my practice slide during these crazy months*. Despite that, he planned to attend the trial every day. "Evan, tell me a little about the project. It's expensive to start up a concert promotion company. You need capital to hold and secure a venue, pay fifty percent down to secure the artists that are to perform, insurance requirements, security personnel, so on, and so forth. I really am going to be tied up the next few weeks with a trial—"

Dex was cut off by the voice on the other end. "Might you be able to squeeze me in possibly tomorrow? My partner will be in town and we'd appreciate the opportunity to meet you."

"How are you around two-thirty??"

"That would be good. How much is your retainer?"

"Hard to say until we speak, then I can quote you a figure after I see what's involved. My hourly rate is $425 per hour, and the first consultation is $400, then we can see if you and I go further."

"Sounds reasonable. See you at two-thirty."

Precisely at 2:30, Nora the receptionist buzzed and stated, "Mr. Dougal and another gentleman are here for their appointment"

"Fine, I'll be right there." Dex had learned early on that clients hated waiting in the reception room, and he made it a point to try to never let a client wait more than ten minutes for a scheduled appointment. It showed the client that his time was important also.

The two men were well dressed in a conservative manner and about mid-fifty in appearance. Articulate and bright, they explained to Dex they were officers of a regionally large

277

financial company and were interested in giving back to the community.

"On the phone you said a portion of the proceeds would go to charity. Is this a nonprofit or not?" Dex asked.

"We thought operating expenses would be paid off in first position, then the remainder would go to use and distribute the money to various schools throughout the five-state region to purchase and wire computers."

Dex discussed setting up a 501(c)(3) not-for-profit corporation. Its advantages as to nontaxable proceeds and the need to establish a budget and business plan. A sound business plan should lay out investment needed, a budget of expenses, working capital requirements and for how long, and much other information. They wanted to keep going, but Dex had given them enough to digest and they needed to do some more homework before their next meeting. Evan pulled a check from his pocket and wanted to write a retainer and get started. In a normal time, Dex would love a client who was ready to write a large check, but he asked for only the consultation fee and promised to send them a written retainer agreement setting forth the terms of the engagement.

The real reason was Dex wasn't sure he wanted to get into a long-range representation until he made up his mind about a number of things, but first he would await the outcome of the trial.

Chapter Fifty-Three

Almost three months later and despite several more delaying tactics of Carpozzi's lawyers, the trial was about to begin. The lawyers had filed several motions to suppress various pieces of evidence, and each motion had to be studied and decided.

Delays were sought because of the voluminous levels of documents that needed to be reviewed. Witness testimony and statements, both good and bad, had to be researched. A trial is like the preparation for a series of battles which ultimately leads to a victory or defeat. During the time of trial, the soldiers or warriors prepare for battle, honing their weapons which instead of armor and firearms are questioning and logical probing to arrive at the truth or, even better, arriving at a point which is to their advantage, even if it's not the truth.

There are rules of engagement, rules of conflict called 'Procedure' and lines of demarcation called 'Rules of Ethical Behavior'.

For those who don't think it's mortal combat, they have never been involved. The warriors or combatants try to convince a judge or jury that their position is the righteous one or that the other side failed to prove their case in point.

The warriors call up reinforcements called 'witnesses' to prove the positions or establish the 'beachheads', from which they can expand the taking of additional territory or move their attack further.

Each additional foothold, hopefully leading to the surrender of the opposition, getting them to make a concession or even better a fatal error, decimates their defenses. A position from which a jury can, with a clear consciousness justify their decision, hopefully based on the facts and not on some psychological or prejudicial thinking arrived at even before they have heard the first shred of evidence.

Add to the war like stake of these trials, a number of additional elements, sex, gambling, celebrities both in the world of recording artists and professional athletes, and crime figures. Yes, in the world today even crime figures can rise to the status of celebrity. You have a circus like atmosphere which requires a tough, confident, intelligent and above reproach like judge to control the courtroom, the press, and keep the players under control.

Judge Allison Maturo was that judge. Born to a middle class Italian family, she knew the streets of Philadelphia. She attended public schools, went to college on an academic scholarship where she waited on tables to earn spending money. Her law school records were also outstanding, graduating in the top five percent of the class.

After graduation, she spent four years working as an assistant DA, trying a variety of cases before opting to leave and enter private practice with a small, but well known criminal defense firm.

Her husband was elected to the House of Representatives and though she was quite qualified, it could not be discounted that her husband's political position had helped her become appointed as one of the youngest federal judges. Against this background, Judge Maturo was determined to prove to the world she had the stature and qualification to preside over such a public trial, keep a tight rein over the proceedings and let the jury come to a fair verdict.

The media both newspaper and television were pressing for all the coverage they could muster, even filing a request for television cameras in the courtroom, which the judge quickly dismissed. 'Let the War Begin' was the headline of one of the daily newspapers on the eve of the first day of the trial. Each trial is a unique happening, but the proceeding moves along fairly established paths.

As the day for the trial began, each side was nervous with anticipation. The defense can request a jury trial and did just that, fearing a judge might not be swayed by any number of factors and with a jury of twelve, it took only one to avoid conviction. From a pool of potential jurors, the jury is picked using a series of questions and examining each potential juror to get those most favorable to your point of view.

Carpozzi had hired expert consultants to research the jury pool, checking their backgrounds, education, age, and other data to try to get someone favorable or at the least not emotional who his lawyers could reach and persuade. Many of the pool had already heard or knew of the case or the celebrities making impartial selection of the panel go very slowly.

Finally came the day for opening statements when the federal prosecutor told the jury what she would prove during the course of the trial. Dex, listening to her opening statement, felt the evidence would certainly convince any rational being of guilt but with juries you never know for sure.

When Carpozzi's attorney gave his opening, he summarily dismissed all that had just been said and spoke to the jury to listen carefully, and when all was said, no way, he concluded, could they find beyond a reasonable doubt the guilt of his client.

Carefully, the government built its case by calling witness after witness, bringing forth a dazzling array of documents and wiretaps, both e-mails and recorded telephone conversations. The defense got their opportunity to cross-examine and attempt to refute the testimony after each witness, but the case was building tighter and tighter.

The testimony of Val retelling the plots to exploit the boxer, the extortion, and blackmail of Q, along with her testimony of the vendetta against Trolly, her tearful telling of her treatment and then the harrowing assault by Sammy crystallized in the minds of the jury the cold and sterile presentation of forensic witnesses. It was her real-life presentation, especially when she broke down on the stand and admitted her part that, the reality of what took place and what Carpozzi and his associates did, made its greatest impression on the jury.

The testimony of the detectives regarding the hit-and-run, the SUV disappearance, and the shock when the detective produced the matching gold-and-diamond cufflink with the one found in Carpozzi's jewelry box in his bedroom, all tied the package heading for what seemed like a forgone conclusion. The guilt and conviction of Vince Carpozzi seemed to be coming.

The defense did on occasion catch a few witnesses in confusion, but for the most part the stories were unbroken.

The lawyers for the defense used a strategy that the government needed to prove beyond a shadow of a doubt the guilt and that it was done and orchestrated by Carpozzi.

Several witnesses testified Carpozzi was home the night of the hit-and-run. The singer who had been promised an audition reluctantly testified she spent the night with Carpozzi, but on cross examination by the prosecution, was unsure of the actual timeline of her appearance.

The night of the assault by Sammy found Carpozzi in Las Vegas and no actual evidence tied him to blackmail and further, the defense made sure the jury understood that he actually lost money on the gambling since Q's team had won the game.

The boxer chose to go with Val of his own accord, and nobody fixed the outcome of the fight.

"Regarding the promotion payoffs, wasn't that the function of record companies to promote their artists?" urged the defense attorney. "Perhaps a promotion man on occasion exceeded his job description by offering a little extra to get some airplay. Certainly that wasn't the fault of Mr. Carpozzi. How could he be responsible for all of the actions of so many independent contractors?" The lawyer looked straight into the eyes of a juror who his expert consultants were sure didn't like the police or federal government. A juror who years before had applied for a federal job and had been turned down. Carpozzi did not take the stand, and in criminal cases there is no legal inference of guilt by his choice not doing so.

After both sides presented their witnesses and introduced their exhibits, it was time for summation and closing arguments.

The government summarized all of its evidence and how it supported a verdict of guilty, describing how Vince Carpozzi was a menace to decent people and needed to be put away. "No one is above the law. You the jury must do your duty," the prosecutor said before quietly taking her seat and looking straight ahead, her heart pounding as she confidently felt there would be a conviction.

The defense attorney took all the evidence and seemed to shred it to uncertainty. "The government has failed to prove my client's guilt beyond a shadow of a doubt, regardless of what they think of Carpozzi as a person. Vincent Carpozzi doesn't have to prove his innocence. The government has to prove his guilt, and that ladies and gentlemen, it has failed to do."

After summations, the judge gets instructions from both sides as to charges he gives to the jury, in effect instructing them on the applicable law that they must apply to the particular case. After instructions from the judge, the jury retires to deliberate all the evidence, finding the facts, reviewing and then when they are ready taking a vote, to determine guilt or innocence. The Carpozzi case was complex, and there were multiple charges, and each had to be deliberated.

The jury holds in its hands the life or death of the defendant and the time during deliberations seems like an eternity.

Carpozzi asked his lawyer, "What do you think?"

"Juries are like a cross section of society. They usually have a nose for the truth, so let's wait and see."

Carpozzi didn't particularly like that response and spoke to another member of the defense team. "Well they have been out five days, and I think it's a good sign. If they were going to convict, it would be done in a hurry."

Conners and Dex met for coffee the fifth morning.

"Jack, what do you think?"

"Doesn't smell right. I thought they would be back by now."

"Yes, but there are a bunch of charges, and it could really take some time to sort it all out."

"We've moved Val and Trolly to a safe place under the Federal Witness Protection Program. They have changed identities with all new cards and been moved to a new state."

"Great, and thanks for all your help. What happens if Carpozzi gets out of this?"

"Not gonna happen, just takes more time for the jury."

Day six: the jury asked for some further instructions from the judge and requested to see the transcripts of the expert witness regarding the payoff to promoters and payola.

Day seven: a note was sent to the judge that they could not come to a unanimous decision.

The judge sent a message to go back and deliberate some more. Two more days passed.

On day ten, a message was sent to the judge that the jury was hopelessly deadlocked at what would later be known to be 10–2.

One juror was now becoming sick and the judge reluctantly declared a mistrial or what is commonly called a 'hung jury'. What happens then depends on what the government wants to do, start over and retry the case, weighing the likelihood of a conviction against the cost to the taxpayers of retrying the case.

"Crap. It's like kissing your sister. After all that work, the SOB gets off for now. We got to start all over." Conners slammed his fist on the court elevator.

"We try him again," the prosecutor said. "Protect those witnesses."

Dex walked out and looked up at the figurine of justice with a blindfold over her eyes. "Justice really is blind as a bat."

Chapter Fifty-Four

The news of the hung jury reached Val and Trolly like the rest of the world by hearing it on the radio.

"What does this mean to us?" said a very disappointed Val.

"We have to be very careful, and Vincent will probably be tried again, but in the meantime, I don't know if he gets out on bail or if he's held in jail until they start the new trial."

"He might come after us."

"That's why we changed our names and identity, and we probably will have protection."

"Do we have to testify again? I can't bear going through that again, and besides, we have to protect Wally. He's so cute and he needs the both of us."

The talk broke off as they held their newborn son up in the air and played with him.

Life for the two of them was now going to be very different. Trolly was given a new name Mark Johnson, a new social security number, driver's license, and even a master's degree in music theory and conducting. This, along with other arrangements set up by the law enforcement agency resulted in Mark getting a teaching job in a state college in Ohio, and Trolly was actually thriving in the position.

He was teaching a music conducting class as well as music composition and a record producing interactive seminar, and the eagerness of his young music-minded students helped take his mind off the many problems still to be worked out. The students marveled at his ability and more than a few wondered who this new professor was and how was he so accomplished.

Val was busy with their son and in setting up house, which gave her an unprecedented feeling of security and comfort. She actually seemed to enjoy this new life, and at least for the time being did not miss the fame and glory of her prior career. Her hair was crimped short and dyed reddish auburn, and with sunglasses and a baseball cap when she went out, she was not readily distinguishable.

The house the government provided was a simple but single detached home on a small and relatively quiet street with large hedges and shrubbery that cut it off from the street.

Other than each other, there were no friends, no family, and even Dex could not get in touch with them.

Mark had been invited to a few college parties from his department, which he mostly skipped and the one or two he attended he did so without Val, now known as Carol, because they were still afraid she might be recognized.

It was too short into the transition to really think how this would play out as the years moved forward. Rather, they chose to not think too far ahead. They enjoyed this almost story-like living and were very doting parents to their young son.

"So how was class today?" she asked one day as she kissed her husband. "Hello."

Trolly laughed. "One of my students told me I should be a real producer and try to get some of my material to a real record company."

"Be careful. What did you say?"

"I told him I wasn't interested and my stuff couldn't make it to the big time."

"Dear, are you okay?" She bent over, kissed, and hugged him.

"Couldn't be better, really. There are days I really miss Dex and talking about my new songs and the business, but you and my boy are the best things that ever happened to me."

"You don't hate me for getting you into this mess?"

"Come here." They were interrupted by the cries of the baby as he awoke from his nap.

"Hey, young man," Trolly said, lifting and hugging his son. "Someday you gonna be the best damn producer and songwriter in the world. How can you miss with your mother's and my genes?"

Dex had returned to his daily practice, but the enjoyment was lacking. He missed his daily conversations with Trolly. A number of his clients felt a different and serious nature in his manner, without the ease and confidence with which he conducted his earlier practice.

Sara had graduated, taken the bar, and, pushed by Dex, was now doing corporate law in a large law firm. On occasion, she would call her ex-boss and they would have a quick lunch and talk about how it had been. His associate, sensing he was not really getting anywhere, had given notice and opted for a small firm in the suburbs. Except for a new secretary, Dex was now on his own.

The boys, while proud of their father had been under a lot of pressure from their classmates because of the notoriety of the trial. Some parents even felt it was unsafe for their kid to play or be around the boys, expecting some calamity.

Donna even noticed her friends cooling toward going out with them, and dinner out with a couple was becoming more and more infrequent. When the dinner table had been cleared, over coffee Donna quietly asked her husband,

"Dex, you seem so pensive and quiet. What do we do?"

"No, I'm alright. It's just I keep waiting for the new trial to start, and truthfully I just don't know. Nothing feels right anymore."

"Maybe we should get away, go on a vacation."

"Donna, what if I wanted to move and start over somewhere? How would you feel?"

"What about the kids? It would be tough for Jamie to miss his senior year in high school."

"Yeah, just a thought. Today I heard a wonderful old song on my Sirius radio, which really made me think. Remember Harry Chapin's song *The Cat in the Cradle?*"

Donna looked at her husband and felt his sadness.

"You know, the father never has time for his son who grows up without much time with his dad. Then the father grows old and his son moves away and has no time for his aging dad. The father suddenly realizes that his son is just like him."

Donna didn't reply and Dex kept on speaking.

"The boys need me, and I'm not being with them very much lately. This case really changed our life, I wonder how

Val and Trolly are making out. They probably are miserable too."

"Are you really that miserable?"

"No, just, eh just, I don't know. Maybe there is something more meaningful to do. Let's table it for now."

"Dad, one of my friends said we could be bombed or shot, so what's the story?" Dex looked at his sons and smiled.

"Come on. We're going through some tough times and we need to stick together and no one is going to hurt you, I promise," Dex replied.

Jamie looked at his mom. "I'd like to move to another place and get out of here. Dad, it's not fair you got us into this." He got up and ran to his room and slammed the door.

Donna looked at Dex. "Go talk to him."

Dex got up and knocked on Jamie's door.

"Please go away. I'm doing homework."

"Son, we need to talk."

Dex entered the room and sat on the bed facing his son. "Sometimes doing the right thing throws you a curve. It's not the easy road to take."

"My friends don't think you're so cool anymore. They say you did bad things and hang with crooks in your practice and we could get murdered or something."

"What? Slow down. I'm the lawyer in this case, not the defendant."

"Yeah, but they say their parents think you were involved, like, in messing up the quarterback and ruining his career. They all saw you on TV with him that night and…"

"What do you think?"

"I don't know. You're my dad. I love you, but—"

291

"No buts. I tried to help my clients, and you know how close I am to Trolly."

"Why did he run away if he's not guilty?"

"He and Val feared their testimony to put an evil person who harmed a lot of people in jail would cause him to try and harm them, and they decided to go away until he was in jail."

"Well if he's so guilty, why did they let him go and not convict him?"

"Sometimes justice works slowly and things need to be worked out."

"Why do my so-called friends pick on me and say mean things about you?"

"Sometimes people project their own fears and prejudices, and sadly it makes them feel stronger to pick on people, but if you know you're right in what you do, then you just face them and move ahead. It's easy to be in a crowd and follow, but sometimes in life you've got to make choices, then hold to your conviction. I had to stick with Val and Trolly, and I know I was right, but I'm so sorry it affected Mom, you, and your brother."

"I love you, Dad."

"I know, son, and I promise it will all work out."

Dex hugged his son and for that moment wished he had never heard of Val or Carpozzi.

Chapter Fifty-Five

It was several months later when the phone rang and Dex heard a familiar voice. "See you in 30 minutes."

"Can you make it forty-five and I'll buy?"

A short time later, Dex, the first to arrive at the diner slid into a booth awaiting Conners.

"Hey, buddy. Good to see you." Conners reached out, and they shook hands.

"What's this I hear about you? Is it true?"

Dex smiled. It seemed as if everybody had heard he was closing his practice and moving to Ohio to accept a professorship his friend the dean had offered. He would be teaching an entertainment course, but also a new course he was developing teaching third-year law students, a combination of ethics and professional business practice.

The dean had given him complete freedom to teach the course anyway he chose, and Dex planned to teach the realities of the real world to graduating students.

Dex had often thought young lawyers left law school and didn't really know what to expect in the practice, and he was determined to show them the light. Perhaps, he'd throw in some of his real-life experiences he'd had in the past two years and how it had changed so many things in his life.

He looked over at his new friend and realized Conners had indeed become a friend.

"I'll miss you and our early breakfasts here, but I won't miss all the turmoil and craziness you bring. What's happening with the case?"

"The feds are reinstituting the case and going after them again. This time the case will be tighter."

"Yeah, and so will the defense."

"Your friends will have to testify again, and by the way, I hear they are doing well and their baby is fine."

"I miss seeing Trolly. He was a really close friend."

"I'm sorry about the way this all turned out. I guess you're making the right choice. Nothing we've heard should cause you any concern. I mean Carpozzi or anybody."

"Jack, I'm not leaving because of Carpozzi. I just realize that my life and that of my family needed to change directions."

"Hey, I didn't mean—"

"I know, but understand, I'm also doing this for my boys as well. They took a beating from their school chums and so-called friends as did my wife."

"I've learned one thing. You don't really know who your real friends are till you really need them. It's surprising some people who you think will stick by you turn and run when trouble comes. Others come up to the plate for you who you would never expect."

"Life can be a pisser."

"Look at me. I couldn't even have a wife in this crazy job. I never know where I'll be assigned or what I'm doing, and most of the time I don't even know who I am or what story I'm making up."

Dex looked at his friend, but before he could say anything, Conners continued. "I am sorry for the way I lied to you early on about my identity and job but I think you understand? You were one of the better things that came out of this experience. Listen, if you ever need anything, just call, and I'll be watching over you and your family and staying in touch. One last thing." He handed Dex a phone number and strange name.

"Wait a week or two when you get to the new town and call this person. Don't ever tell anyone about this 'cause I would lose my job, and don't lose the paper."

Dex looked at the paper, a little puzzled but asked no questions.

"Good luck to you, and make sure they put that sucker away this time."

"Don't be too hard on your students. They didn't ask for you." Conners smiled, got up, and walked away.

Dex looked at his friend. "I'm not walking away, just changing directions," he whispered to himself.

Chapter Fifty-Six

Dex sat in the den of his new house. It was comfortable. Bookcases lined one wall, and on the opposite wall to his desk, he had hung platinum albums and framed jerseys of a few of his clients. There was a fireplace and his favorite lounging chair, which was placed equidistant between his sound system and large-screen TV. The house was a single detached with charm and grace. A sliding glass door led to a terrace overlooking an enclosed yard. It was cozy, but not what he had back on the main line of Philadelphia.

It's crazy, but isn't that what life really is? he thought. Dex poured himself a glass of sherry, leaned back, and mused, *Who would ever guess it would be this way?*

A little over a year ago he was a busy lawyer in a bustling practice and now he was beginning a professorship in a small Ohio college town.

Val, a multi-platinum recording artist, was virtually in hiding with a son and her husband, a well-regarded producer and songwriter, who was teaching music theory. They, at least according to Conners, were happy with their lives.

Carpozzi was in limbo awaiting his retrial with half of the government agencies hot in pursuit, and for sure he was not very happy.

Dex didn't know whether he was happy or just escaping from the notoriety and publicity. Funny, he thought at one point publicity good or bad was what a lawyer wanted. It helped to network, but what he hadn't counted on was the toll it had taken on his sons and wife. Life was cruel sometimes, and the people who least deserved trouble got double doses, not of their own doing. Perhaps, that above all was why Dex pulled up his practice and changed directions and life for the sake of his innocent family.

"Who would have ever thought this would be?" he said to his drink and swallowed the remainder.

"Hey, Dad, can I talk to you a minute?"

"Sure, Jamie, what's up?"

Dex looked at his son who would next fall be heading to college.

"Mom says it's alright with her, but I should ask you anyway. Can Lisa come to dinner with us?"

"Lisa?"

"You know, I told you about her last night. She's the girl who's in my class and lives down the block."

"Sure, Son, of course." Dex smiled to himself. At least Jamie liked the move.

Dex got up and looked for Brett, finding him in his room. "Hey, Son, what's happening? Want to throw the football?"

"No thanks, Dad. I'm watching TV."

"You okay?"

"Not really. Why did we have to move? I don't like this new school, and the kids are creeps."

"Son, you've got to give it time. Look at Jamie, he has a girlfriend already. I know it's not easy leaving your friends, but in time everything will work out. Come on let's go outside."

Later that night, Dex found Donna staring out the window looking at nothing in particular. The move had been tough on Donna, and she never let her emotions or real thoughts be paramount to her husband's situation.

She had understood Dex was standing by Trolly and Val, but she was confused and hurt by the reaction of her so-called friends.

She never accepted the reaction of a couple of friends who literally shunned her when Dex got the negative publicity. Most of all, she felt the tremendous hurt her husband carried but never expressed. She knew he was a great lawyer, a wonderful father and husband, yet she was unsure if the move was the right thing to do.

Dex walked over and gently placed his hands on her shoulder and hugged her.

"I love you, and thanks for being you. I could never have made it without your support."

"Are we going to be alright?"

"Of course we will. You'll see. I need you to stay strong. Hey, that Lisa is really cute. Our kids are growing up," Dex said, trying to change the subject. Donna didn't answer, just stared out the window at a strange street and stranger life.

Chapter Fifty-Seven

Dex had nearly forgotten the name and number Conners had given him in the diner. Sitting in his den, he had been going through some papers he had bunched together prior to the move and was idly cleaning the package of papers when he found the slip. He remembered that Conners was very mysterious and told him to wait two weeks before calling.

The name meant nothing to him, but he decided to call. "Hello." The answering voice sounded vaguely familiar, but a telephone apparatus, which disguised the voice threw him off for a moment, until his heart started to pound. "Is that really you? Don't answer, it's Dex. Where are you? I'm teaching at the law school and living on Magnolia Point about ten minutes from the school, moved out here with Donna and the kids. Be well."

Dex hung up, fearing that if his phone was tapped they could possibly trace the call and not wishing to put his friend in any more danger than he already was. He was just happy to know Trolly was alive somewhere.

He decided against telling Donna about the call—the less known the better.

Donna and Dex were home one evening getting the Christmas decorations out and planning to trim the tree. Dex was in charge of wrapping the lights around the tree and making sure the lights worked. Donna was with the kids in charge of the decorations. This was a pizza night at the Randle home, and Dex was hoping the Christmas trimming would ease the tension of the move.

"There's the door. It must be the pizza," chimed Brett.

"I'll get it," Dex answered as he moved to open the door.

"Merry Christmas," said a short-haired redhead holding a young boy by the hand. Then he saw Trolly, looking a lot older with a gray head of hair and gray beard.

They grabbed each other as Dex pulled them in and shut the door.

"And who might this young man be? I'll bet he would like a candy cane, if his mother lets him have it." Dex picked up the little boy and called for Donna who instantly recognized Val, and they burst into tears as they hugged and seemed to dance around.

"Oh he's gorgeous, he has your eyes," Donna said, taking hold of the child.

"How did you find us and how did you get out?"

Trolly looked at Dex but didn't say anything.

"What are you doing here? I thought you were in hiding." Donna had so many questions, but quickly shifted her attention to Wally and offered him a cupcake, which ended the questions for the moment.

They couldn't believe that Trolly was teaching at the same university where Dex would be teaching. Dex smiled and thought back to his friend Conners who he decided must be the President in disguise—that man really could pull strings. "How did he arrange this?"

When they settled in and washed down the pizza with a couple of beers, Trolly explained what they had been going through and how they were in fear of Carpozzi finding them.

"In spite of everything we really are much happier now, but I do miss producing. At least the ringing in my ears is one constant note. Do you really ever think, this will end and we can resume our lives?"

Without waiting for an answer, Trolly looked at Dex. "Man, I'm really sorry for all this has caused you and Donna."

"Don't be crazy. I've been thinking about this move for a couple of years, and besides, maybe one day if teaching law isn't for me, I'll convince Jerry to quit as dean and we can start a law firm."

"I'll always be indebted for what you did for Val and me."

"Cut it out and let me get you another beer."

"No, man, we've got to get back, and I've had my limit. It's not like the old days. I've got to teach tomorrow."

"I'll be in touch," Dex said.

"No, I think it's better if I call you, but we will get together again—real soon."

"Val, I love your hair short and the red…"

"Forget it, but thanks anyway."

"No kidding. It does look good."

They all hugged, Trolly, Val, and their son got their coats and walked out into the cold evening air as Dex watched from the window.

Was this real or was it a dream? Dex hoped he would wake up and everything would be back two years or so. "Tick tock. Tick tock, the hands of time move on, down upon some

301

unsuspecting child and soon enough they will all be old," Dex mumbled to himself. Where will it all end?

Chapter Fifty-Eight

Donna reached across the counter and poured a cup of coffee for her husband.

"I don't remember ever seeing you more nervous, even at the trial. What's wrong?"

"Guess it's first day jitters for my first class."

"You've taught many times before. You'll be fine. Just stay natural."

"How do I look?"

"Like a law school professor with your wireless glasses and a tweed jacket, but if you want my honest opinion take off the jeans and put on a pair of khakis."

"Too much?"

"Change them and please relax."

Dex bounded the stairs two at a time, changed, and when he returned, kissed his wife and walked toward the front door.

"You look much better," Donna called after him. "I love you, call me later."

Dex entered the old but classic building that housed the law school and walked down the hall.

"Morning, Professor Randle," one of the students mumbled as he passed in the hall.

Knocking on the door to the dean's office, Dex paused, then went in to find his friend Jerry already hard at work, going over some budgetary spreadsheets.

Jerry looked up and smiled. "Well, Professor, you ready?"

"I think so."

"Great to have you on board. Let's grab some lunch when you finish."

"Here goes."

The classroom was like so many others, a podium up front and a semicircle of rows with swivel desk chairs and microphones on top of each desk. The classroom could hold about sixty, but this third-year elective course on entertainment law was limited to just thirty. Most students were already seated, and the majority sat with laptop computers open and ready to go.

Dex moved up the two steps onto the stage, placed his notes on the lectern of the podium and looked at the class, momentarily thinking it looked like a nice bunch of eager students pretty evenly divided between men and women. He smiled. "Good morning. Nice to be here. I'm Dex Randle, and as many of you already know, I practiced entertainment and sports law and was an adjunct professor before the dean asked me to join the faculty." He paused. So far they seemed to be listening. "What we'll do this semester is examine the law as it relates to athletes and entertainers. I hope to make it a practical course for you, and I will use the Socratic approach, ask some questions and expect you to be prepared with the week's assignment. I want class participation, so ask questions and feel free to ask anything, even if it goes beyond course material."

A hand shot up. "Professor, will we cover any of the trials you and your clients were involved with?"

Dex paused for a moment. *Boy, was that fast, right out of the box*, he thought. He waited to respond as if he were being tested right from the start. "Yes, I'm here to teach and you to learn, so anything is fair game. You know in just six to eight months, you'll be graduating, and the reality of the law will really be different from school, and if I can help bridge that gap, then I have achieved my purpose.

"Your question made me recall what a great American author James Baldwin wrote, 'The price one pays for pursuing any profession, or calling, is an intimate knowledge of its ugly side.'"

Dex paused and looked at the students who were now in rapt attention and taking notes. "Yes, we will examine not only the ethics and proper ways to practice but also the ugly side of this profession as well." He stopped for a moment, reached into his jacket pocket, pulled out a yellow stick-um package, and handed each student a sticky note.

When he returned to the podium, the class was buzzing about this new professor, and they were loving the class already.

"Now, not in your notes or computer 'cause whatever I say will be studied a few days before the exam and then discarded, but on the yellow stick-um, I'm about to give you eight magic words I want you to print on the stick-um and memorize. These words, which you really won't fully understand right now, but you will as the years pass, should be pasted on your makeup mirrors or shaving mirrors or phone pads, so you can always think about them before doing something wrong or perhaps being talked into something you shouldn't do by a client or even a partner.

"Are you ready for the eight words?" Dex paused as they leaned forward in anticipation, and he suddenly knew he had made the right choice.

THE PRACTICE OF LAW IS FRAUGHT WITH PERIL.

The new beginning.